Nain Rouge:
Book III: The Red Truth

by: josef bastian

illustrations by: bronwyn coveney

"Nain Rouge: the Red Truth" Copyright © 2014 Josef Bastian
All rights reserved
Illustrations by Bronwyn Coveney Copyright © 2014
ISBN-13: 978-1499226799
ISBN-10: 1499226799
Printed and bound by Createspace Publishing
Body text in 12-point Arno Pro with 18-point lead.
Chapter titles in 25-point Blackadder ITC.
Cover design and book layout by Matthew Sakey and Carl Winans
First printing.

Stories to be shared.

Honi soit qui mal y pense

(Spurned be the one who thinks evil of it)

Prologue

Most **Folktellers understand** the importance of history. We love to weave events from the past into the stories that we tell. A famous general named Santayana once said, "Those that forget history are doomed to repeat it."

That's some good advice that we would do well to remember. Frankly, I think history has a way of hiding and revealing the truth about almost everything. This applies to both human beings and magical creatures. Take the Nain Rouge and Antoine de la Mothe Cadillac for example. Who would have thought that one, small, seemingly insignificant interaction would change the course of history forever?

And it's that event that seems like a wonderful place to return to our story.

The forty-two year old explorer stood in the Paris crowd that had gathered at a party in his honor. Antoine de la Mothe Cadillac moved slowly about the room, mingling with disinterest and subtle aloofness.

It was April, 1700 and Cadillac had already spent too much time in France, trying to convince the king to let him build a settlement near the straits between the Great Lakes. He had finally gotten his wish and was now anxious to get back to the Americas.

Antoine was a restless soul. He never could settle down completely and his joy was found in discovery, exploration and conquering the unknown. It was this restlessness that he had to keep in check as he shook the hands of his countrymen, made small talk and smiled with all the sincerity of a floating crocodile in a stagnant swamp.

Cadillac worked his way toward the outskirts of the palace ballroom. As he turned to greet another admirer, he came face to face with a fortune teller. Performers had been hired to entertain the party guests with magic tricks, juggling and various other marvellous acts. The fortune teller had been wandering about the ballroom, reading palms and forecasting future events for the delighted Parisians.

The small, dark-eyed woman instinctively took the explorer's hand and was met with no resistance. Cadillac watched as she ran her forefinger along the creases in his right palm. The fortune teller shuddered a little as she looked back up at the explorer.

~ 5 ~

"Beware the Nain Rouge…" she whispered in a raspy, ominous voice.

Cadillac smiled uncomfortably, "Silly woman, what do you mean by this?"

"The Red Dwarf. Appease him, show him respect and honor. If you fail to do so, it is at your own peril."

Antoine de la Mothe Cadillac quickly pulled his hand away. He stared down at the fortune teller with a diminishing look of surprise and slight confusion. After a brief, awkward moment of silence, he chuckled loudly so that it appeared he was slightly amused by the whole affair.

The crowd chuckled with him as he shook his head gently, waved an affectionate goodbye and made his way out into the cool Paris evening.

Chapter 1
Into the Storm

"**Mom, you just** don't get it!" Lynni yelled with a hoarse, raspy longing in her voice.

"Oh, I do get it Lynni, that is exactly why you are not going," her mother replied calmly, yet firmly.

"They need me… I promised… I have to go! Don't you trust me?" Lynni pleaded.

"Lynni," her father spoke in a very serious and quiet tone, "We have been through this with you all week. This is not an issue of whether or not we trust you. Of course we trust you. Our decision is really based on keeping you safe; it is as simple as that. You've been through so much already. Your mom and I aren't ready to put you back in harm's way."

There was a brief moment of silence as the gears turned inside Lynni's head; she readied herself for her next attack in their extensive argument. Slowly, she got up from the living room couch and circled around her parents until she was facing them.

Instead of yelling hysterically or crying her eyes out, Lynni sat down on the edge of the coffee table and leaned forward toward her parents with silent seriousness.

"Mom, Dad, it's really important that you understand where I'm coming from. I know that you spoke with Dr. Beele and he gave you all of the gory details about the Nain Rouge and why this trip was so important for everybody, but he didn't tell you what it means to me."

Lynni's parents looked at each other with a renewed sense of worry. They had never seen their daughter appear so serious and foreboding. Her mother couldn't help but lean forward and rub her daughter's knee in comfort and reassurance.

Lynni took a deep breath, sighed slightly and began to speak, "What Dr. Beele couldn't have told you was how I felt when Lutin was inside of me…it was as if he stole something, part of my soul. When I was possessed, I felt such darkness, such a deep, heavy evil that I thought I would suffocate from the weight of his anger. When he finally let go, it felt like a little piece of me was missing, like he took something away and left an empty space in my heart."

Lynni's parents were silent as stones and didn't interrupt her as she continued, "That's why I have to go with them. I need to get back what he took from me, the part of me that's missing."

To say that Lynni's parents were stunned would be the understatement of the century. They had never heard their daughter speak with so much power and conviction. There was no whining or complaining in her voice, only the deep-seeded knowledge that this journey was one she had to make, no matter what the cost.

Lynni's mom was the first to speak after a brief moment of awkward silence, "I'm at a loss, here, Lynni. We're dealing with things that are beyond the normal parenting things your father and I are used to."

"Your mom is right, sweetie," her dad added, "This whole

~ 9 ~

situation is really hard to take in all at once."

Her mother continued, "But the one thing we do know is that we believe you. We believe everything that you have told us and we're so thankful that you've been so open and honest with us."

Both parents looked at their daughter with a deep, heart-felt reassurance, as if to say that even though they didn't have all of the answers, things would eventually work out for the best.

"So, I can go?" Lynni asked directly without missing a beat in the conversation.

Lynni's mom and dad looked at each other and then back at her. They did not say a word but nodded their heads slightly.

"Oh, thank you! Thanks so much you guys!" Lynni jumped up with renewed excitement. "Thanks for believing in me. You know that this is something I have to do."

Her parents smiled quietly and nodded again. With that, Lynni jumped up from the edge of the coffee table and ran upstairs to get everything ready for her journey. As she raced up the steps to her room, her parents remained seated in the living room, almost frozen with the knowledge that they had just agreed to send their daughter into the darkness of unknown dangers. All they could do now was hope and pray for the best.

Chapter 2
The First Leg

The van had barely entered Marshall, Michigan when Lynni finished telling the story of her surprise appearance in the darkness of the school parking lot. Tom, Elly, AJ, Vic and Dr. Beele were all surprised at her parents' change of heart at the last minute.

"Basically, they said they trusted me and they understood that this was a trip that I had to make," Lynni said as she ended her story.

"We're all glad that you're here, Lynni," Elly smiled confidently.

"Yeah," Tom added, "We had no idea how much Lutin had messed with your insides…"

Elly elbowed Tom in the ribs, giving him the stink eye - that look that said to stop being so blunt and unfeeling.

"Uh, what I meant to say was that we know how you feel. We've all been there…and we're all here to help, OK?"

Lynni smiled at all of them. She knew she had made the right decision.

As the conversation waned, Dr. Beele pointed out that the DIA van was now traveling through Marshall, Michigan, and informed them that the city marked the midpoint between Detroit and Chicago. It rose to greet the excited travelers in all of its 19th century glory, as they glided down Michigan Avenue, through its picturesque streets and past its stately homes and mansions. The children felt a strange sense of excitement and energy as they passed through the town. It was an odd sort of static electricity that ran through each of them.

"You can probably feel the energy around here, can't you?" Dr. Beele questioned from the driver's seat of the van.

The teens looked at each other, wondering if Dr. Beele was also a mind reader. How did he know what they were feeling?

As they drove through town, Dr. Beele pointed out that Marshall was intersected by Michigan Avenue, the old military road than ran from Detroit to Chicago. Though the new interstates that were built in the 1950's and 60's now by-passed many of these old trails, Marshall remained directly in the path of this historical, horizontal line. The group was, in fact, traveling directly along one of the ley lines that Dr. Beele had mentioned to them previously. These were the energy lines in the pattern that Lutin had been connecting over the past few months. Michigan Avenue ran right through the Nain Rouge's power grid.

"That energy you feel is from the ley line we are on," Beele shouted from the front. "This is one of the lines that connects the lower waterways of the Great Lakes to all the great cities where the lines intersect. That wobbly feeling will subside once we get back onto Interstate 94."

Beele's brief description of the energy grid was a quick wake-up call to the entire group. They had been so caught up in Lynni's story, that they had forgotten why they came on this trip in the first place. By feeling those initial electric vibrations, they were gently zapped back into the reality of their situation. They were on a mission; a mission to stop the Nain Rouge from completing his energy grid and controlling

~ 13 ~

the land and water with his evil power.

With that common dark thought now fresh in their brains, the team noticed, once again, that Hieronymus Beele was right. Sure enough, once the van reached the city limits and got back onto the interstate, the jittery, electric sensation subsided and the group's sense of calm and relaxation returned. They were back on track to Chicago.

The name "Chicago" was first recorded in 1688 in a French document, where it appears as Chigagou, an Algonquian word meaning "onion field". The document stated that wild onion and garlic grew profusely in the area. Now, hundreds of years later, this small band of adventurers was headed toward the same swamps, marshes and fields, unaware of the strange smells that were growing heavy in the air around them.

"Dr. Beele," Elly spoke up once the van was back underway on the interstate, "Where are we stopping first, once we get to Chicago?"

Beele peeked at Elly in the rearview mirror and smiled slightly, "Our first stop is the Museum of Science and Industry. Once there, we will call on the curator and fellow Knight of the Order, Ms. Margaret Anne Bellflower."

"What does she have to do with the Nain Rouge?" AJ asked with growing interest.

"Much," Beele replied curtly but respectfully. "She is well aware of our predicament and stands at the ready to help us in our quest. I just hope that we can get there in time to do what needs to be done."

With that, the doctor went silent and re-focused his attention on the road in front of him. The teens had grown used to Beele's vague and often ominous statements, like the last one. So, instead of piling worry upon worry, they silently agreed to just enjoy each other's company for the rest of the trip. After all, even though they were entering deep water, they were all in the same boat. Being together meant more than anything.

Chapter 3
A Dark Palace in the White City

The *foundation of* every city is people. Wherever people gather together to live, conduct business and grow, cities will form. In

these places, everything multiplies upon itself. As more people arrive, cities grow in size and complexity, encapsulating all that is good and evil within the brick, concrete and heart of every citizen. Within this flux of growth and change, once in a while, all of these forces come together in a physical manifestation so grand, that its impact lingers on over the centuries.

The World's Columbian Exposition opened to the general public on May 1, 1893 in Chicago, Illinois. The fair was launched as a tribute to Christopher Columbus's 400th anniversary of discovering the western world.

They called it the White City. All of the great buildings had been painted white, and the streets were lined with the new technology of electric light. It created a stark contrast to the gray, low-lying buildings that slumped deeper within the inner city.

From May until October of that year, the exposition covered more than 600 acres, featuring nearly 200 new buildings of classical architecture, canals, lagoons, and people and cultures from around the world. Over 27 million people (almost half of the U.S. population at the time) attended the exposition, which became a symbol of the emerging industrial might and power of America.

But despite this great expression of innovation and light at the turn of the century, the fairgrounds proved to be a magnet for the shadowy side of the human soul. This great gathering attracted the likes Dr. H. H. Holmes, a silent, serial killer, who quietly took the lives of dozens of unsuspecting women and children. Using the fair as a distracting backdrop for his mayhem, the "good doctor" disposed of any guilt or evidence in a custom furnace in the basement of his own office building.

Holmes cast an eerie shadow over the White City. His dark deeds seeped into the land and water, and were in stark contrast to the joyful energy created by a world's fair that showcased such great potential and hope of a people on the threshold of the twentieth century.

Holmes was not the only evil lurking in the White City. As Mayor Carter Harrison, Sr. prepared to conclude the exposition, he was assassinated by Patrick Eugene Prendergast, only two days before the falling of the final curtain. Prendergast claimed he had been slighted by the mayor, overlooked for a position within the mayor's administration. Ultimately, the closing ceremonies were cancelled.

This energy permeated the ground now. It flowed within the water that surrounded Chicago. Smack dab in the middle of this play between light and darkness was the Palace of Fine Arts. The south entrance, which faced the center of the fairgrounds, could only be approached by boat from a greenish-blue lagoon. The great building housed famous works of art for the fair. The building was so large, that it was said that to spend only one minute at each exhibit, would take a fairgoer twenty-six days.

Truly, this was fertile ground for the powers of humanity – energy both good and evil.

When the Columbian Exposition of 1893 ended, decay set in. The Palace sat abandoned for almost thirty years, and fell into ruin. The other great buildings were either moved, burned or torn down. It was not until the 1930's when the Palace of Fine Arts was resurrected to its former glory. It soon became the permanent home for the Museum of Science and Industry, housing the history, the hope and all too often the unseen hatred that bleeds through the dual nature of our humanity.

The Nain Rouge felt quite welcome at this intersection of ley lines, in a city so rich with darkness that it rippled beneath the water and saturated its swampy ground.

Chapter 4
Lutin's Trail

The *marshland that* surrounded Chicago had been rising for weeks. Throughout the country, the water table around lakes, rivers and oceans had been steadily increasing for months. Flooding had become common in these late winter months, as thousands of people were losing their homes every week.

To make matters worse, the rising tides brought with them an invasive and dangerous fish. No one really knew how these strange fish had gotten into the river. Some say that they were dumped there by bored collectors. Others say they came into the water from bilge tanks on international freighters. But for most, the rising waters and these foreign invaders remained a great, dark mystery. Asian carp were moving north, up from the Mississippi River. They could grow to be up to 100 pounds and could jump eight to ten feet in the air. The fear was that they would soon be migrating into the Great Lakes, killing off smaller fish and destroying the fishing and gaming industries for years to come.

These fears led the U.S. Army Corps of Engineers to construct an electric barrier in the Chicago Sanitary and Ship Canal, the only aquatic link between the Great Lakes and the Mississippi River drainage basins. Fish were now being electrocuted to prevent them from entering the lakes.

A brief news article last Friday, mentioned that when the barriers were activated, a small, odd-looking man was seen tampering with the power grid near the mouth of the canal. The article stated:

"Officials noted a temporary malfunction of a barrier that left the

lakes vulnerable for a few minutes. When security went to investigate, they found only traces of potential human tampering – small footprints near the banks of the canal. One officer did report hearing a distant, odd laughter and the faint smell of sulphur near the area in question."

AJ read the article aloud to the rest of the van as they continued their way toward Chicago. "This sounds like Lutin's work," AJ stated, half under his breath.

"It certainly does sound like something the Nain Rouge would find great pleasure in," Dr. Beele responded, unaware that AJ was only talking to himself and didn't really mean for anyone to hear.

Lynni added, "It's not really a surprise, is it? I mean, it's what we are here for right – to stop him?"

"That is precisely why we are here," Beele responded firmly. "Yeah, but I wonder sometimes Doc. Are we following him or is he following us?"

Tom looked over at Elly with a knowing glance. It was as if they could almost communicate telepathically now. All that they had been through together had created a subconscious bond between the two teens.

Elly turned around in her bench seat and looked directly at Vic, "I think the answer is a little of both, Vic."

~ 22 ~

"Huh?" Vic replied, a bit puzzled.

"What she's saying," Tom piped in, "Is that Lutin can be anywhere at any time. Now that he's free, he can go wherever he wants, whenever he wants."

Elly added, "I think he knows that we are following him and he is definitely following us. It's all a game to him…a sick, twisted, dark game."

"That may all be true," the curator interjected, "but we have one, small advantage over Lutin. The Nain Rouge may know that he's being followed, but he could not know for what purpose. Remember, absolute power corrupts absolutely.

"What's that supposed to mean?" Vic wondered aloud from the back of the van.

"What it means, Vic," Beele yelled over his back shoulder, "is that Lutin believes he can't be stopped, which leaves him open to our plans to stop him."

These words had an oddly calming effect on the entire group. A gentle quiet settled over the teens as they pondered Dr. Beele's words once again. Each of them wondered what they were really getting themselves into.

The Ford Econoline van had reached the marshes that surrounded the city and in the distance, they could begin to make out the shapes and angles of the magnificent Chicago skyline. Interstate 94 rose out of the swampy grasses, wrapping its way around Lake Michigan and unfolding itself right into the heart of downtown Chicago. The late winter wind whipped around the van. The Hawk was strong and menacing that day. The wind in Chicago was so famous, it even had its own name. Natives called it "Hawkins" or the "Hawk" and would comment on particularly blustery days, "Hawkins is really out today." This was one of those days.

In just a few exits, they would be at the Museum of Science and Industry, the welcome and honored guests of Ms. Margaret Anne Bellflower.

Chapter 5
A Bellflower

Three docents came running down the great north steps of the museum. They made a beeline toward the van full of Michiganders. Dr. Beele made sure the doors of the van were locked as the three strangers began to pound violently on the driver's side window.

"What the heck is going on?" Vic yelled from the back of the vehicle. Lynni, AJ, Tom and Elly echoed his sentiment, as they all braced themselves against their seats.

"I am not quite sure," Beele retorted with a curt, nervousness that was very out of character for the usually subdued curator, "but we will certainly find out shortly."

Beele acknowledged the person pounding on his door by rolling down his window ever so slightly. He smiled at the man and nodded at the others standing by his side. He then waited patiently to see what this anxious group had to say.

"Dr. Beele?" they asked frantically.

"Yes, I am Hieronymus Beele, how may I be of service?"

"Dr. Beele," an unknown woman stepped up, "we've been expecting you, all of you. But things are happening – we need you – Dr. Bellflower sent us to get you. Please, come with us quickly!"

Beele looked back at the children and nodded his head. Without even knowing their names, he knew he could trust these people. The doctor unlocked the doors and instructed the group to follow the docents into the Museum of Science and Industry.

Leaving the van right where it was, the entire entourage made their way rapidly up the museum steps, leaving the DIA vehicle in the

~ 26 ~

middle of the museum's circular driveway.

Upon entering the great brass doors of the museum's main entrance, Dr. Beele, Tom, Elly, AJ, Lynni and Vic stopped dead. The museum was in shambles and Dr. Bellflower was nowhere to be found.

One of the docents spoke up, "We found the museum this way when we came into work this morning. We had to shut down for the day."

Lynni looked up above the main door. The mission statement for the museum was supposed to read, "To inspire the inventive genius in everyone." But someone had spray-painted over the word *"inspire"* and scrawled *"DESTROY"* underneath it.

"Whoa! What the heck happened in here?" Vic gasped under his breath.

In a very serious tone, Hieronymus turned his attention to one of the nameless docents and asked, "Where is Dr. Bellflower?"

"The last I saw her, she was checking out the other exhibits for further damage. She told us to keep watch for you by the front door."

With that, Dr. Beele ran deeper into the museum, the teens following close behind. As they passed through each chamber and room of the museum, it was clear to them that much had been disturbed. The odd thing was not how much damage there was, but rather what had actually been damaged. The vandalism was not one of rage or uncontrollable anger. It seemed like the destruction was quite cold and calculated, executed with great precision and determination.

The small group called out Dr. Bellflower's name as they made their way into the deeper recesses of the darkened museum. They stepped into the unlit space that housed Colleen Moore's Miniature Fairy Castle. This elaborate miniature house was created by silent film star Colleen Moore in the 1930s, and was donated to the Museum of Science and Industry in 1949.

As they shined their small flashlights into the exhibit, they could see the miniature mansion in complete disarray. The little chairs were stacked on top of each other forming a tiny pyramid. The golden cups, jeweled goblets and silver plates that had been set at the large table in the banquet hall no longer rested in their place settings. Instead, it appeared that all of the dinnerware had been glued to the ceiling, along with all of the faux food…turkey, mutton, waxed fruit and cranberry sauce included.

Oddly enough, throughout the castle, nothing seemed to be broken, just re-arranged and misplaced in a methodical, mischievous manner. The adventurers shook their heads in confusion at the oddity, and made their way into the next exhibit hall.

The greatest surprise came when they turned the corner and

entered the gallery housing a giant World War II submarine. The U505 submarine that had been captured from the Germans in World War II loomed in front of them. But it was not right-side-up like it was supposed to be. No, the submarine was standing up on its propellers, completely vertical from floor to ceiling! The underwater vessel looked like giant, steel cocoon that was ready to burst open to reveal a mammoth moth or butterfly. Its shadow was so large that it cast another layer of darkness upon the dark that already permeated the exhibit hall. They knew that this great war machine could fall on them at any minute, crushing the entire team with one, mighty blow, but they couldn't worry about that right now, because there in the exhibit, in the low light of morning, they saw Margaret Anne Bellflower, lying full-length across the center of the floor. Next to the curator, squatted a red, grinning creature that seemed to be whispering something into her ear.

Beele's stomach dropped at the sight of this twisted, bizarre picture. The whole scene looked like one of his paintings that hung in the DIA galleries; a painting by Fuseli, called *The Nightmare*, which depicted a sleeping woman lying down on a bed with a dark troll-like creature sitting on her chest.

Now, this horrific image was illustrated for real, right in front of his own eyes. It was Lutin, reveling in the chaos that he had created,

~ 29 ~

sitting right beside Dr. Beele's friend and colleague. In this odd, twisted moment, time stood still. The curator from Detroit and his young friends stood silently in the doorway, staring at the scene that seemed to hang before them like a giant, grotesque portrait. In this frozen moment, a wispy, shivering sound rose from Lutin. Lutin looked over at the group and smiled wickedly. His lips did not move, but a strange musical noise, almost like the faint pulses of a calliope elevated to the ceiling of the great exhibit hall. Slowly swirling through the air came the foreboding sing-song:

> *"So on his Nightmare through the evening fog*
> *Flits the squab Fiend o'er fen, and lake, and bog;*
> *Seeks some love-wilder'd maid with sleep oppress'd,*
> *Alights, and grinning sits upon her breast."*

A sick churning began to roll in Beele's stomach. He recognized these words. They came from beneath an etching of *The Nightmare* painting that hung in the DIA. The Nain Rouge was mocking them and enjoying every minute of it.

Lynni was the only one from the entire group that didn't hesitate. As soon as she saw Lutin next to Dr. Bellflower, she began running directly toward them. On sheer instinct, she knew that she had to separate the Nain Rouge from the museum curator if there was any hope of Dr. Bellflower surviving. Lynni was running at full speed toward the odd pair, ready to pull Lutin off of the good doctor, but as soon as she reached out to grab the sinister little troll, he disappeared in a plume of yellowy, sulphuric smoke, cackling wildly in an echo that soon faded away.

"Dr. Bellflower, are you alright?" Lynni whispered, as she knelt beside her.

The Chicago curator stirred a little but did not sit up right away. Everything had happened so fast. Dr. Beele was still standing in the open archway with Tom, Elly, AJ and Vic. They were all sort of stunned and frozen by Lynni's actions. Each one felt a little sorry that they didn't follow her right away.

In the calm that followed, the rest of the team caught up with Lynni and hovered quietly around Margaret Anne Bellflower. They stared down at the dazed curator with great concern and wonder. After what seemed like an eternity, Dr. Bellflower began to come around.

Dr. Beele had warned the teens not to try to lift her, just in case she had suffered some sort of head or neck injury. His precautions were warranted but unnecessary, as Dr. Bellflower finally sat up under her own power.

"What happened here?" Dr. Bellflower said in a raspy voice, "Who has done this to my museum?"

"Maggie, please," Dr. Beele replied in a hushed, comforting tone, "rest easy now, dear, everything is alright now…"

The teenagers had never heard Dr. Beele speak so tenderly before. He was always controlled and calm, but now the tone of his voice seemed to be filled with a depth and emotion that only comes with the love and affection for someone who holds a place close to your heart.

"I'm fine, Hieronymus, really." Dr. Bellflower responded as she lifted herself off of the floor. "I am just very curious as to what happened. I was opening the museum for the day when everything started going haywire. I heard loud noises, objects and exhibits started flying around and then…and then *it* appeared."

"What appeared?" Vic stepped up and asked.

Dr. Bellflower continued, as she brushed the dust off of her dress slacks, "I'm not sure, really. It was a little red creature. He was hopping around the exhibit hall, laughing, cackling and mumbling to himself as everything went flying about. Then he looked at me…directly at me…"

The curator shuddered and began to fall back again, as if the recent memory of her horrible experience was just too much for her to bear. Fortunately, Dr. Beele and Elly reacted to her swooning and caught her mid-fall.

Tom and Elly knew exactly what she was talking about. They had the same experience when they were on their 7th grade field trip to the DIA, when they first encountered the Nain Rouge and got sucked into his deep, dark stare. They both passed out as well, waking up in dizzy confusion. Tom and Elly had no idea at the time how much their lives would change because of that one, terrible moment.

Dr. Bellflower regained her composure, "I'm fine now…As I was saying, he looked at me and after a while, I felt as if I was being pulled into his gaze, almost as if I was being hypnotized. I felt nauseous and then everything went dark. When I awoke, this young lady was tending to me. That is all I can remember."

"We have much to share with you Maggie," Dr. Beele stated as calmly and as matter-of-factly as he could. "Is there a place where we can all sit down and chat?"

"Yes, my office is quite comfortable and there is plenty of room for all of you. Please, follow me."

Dr. Bellflower guided the group through the darkened rooms of the museum, avoiding or jumping over objects and artifacts that had been upset or overturned in the chaos as they went.

No one said a word during this short journey. Everyone was on guard wondering what may happen next as they slipped deeper into the dangerous unknown.

Chapter 6
Secrets Revealed

Margaret Anne Bellflower's office was decorated in complete contrast to her colleague's in Detroit. A bright blue, modern cloth sectional couch angled itself in the corner of the room, while a narrow, stylish European desk had been situated in front of a large, picture window that brought warm light into the entire environment.

A number of sleek chairs made of light wood and metal had been positioned around a large, circular table, indicating Dr. Bellflower had been ready for the arrival of her visitors. In the center of the table, sat a beautiful tea service. Tom and Elly looked over at each other, while the rest of party was still scanning the room. The tea set looked very familiar. In fact, upon closer inspection, Tom and Elly realized that it was an exact duplicate of the teapot, cups, saucers and tray that they had used in Dr. Beele's office back at the DIA. Elly smiled at Tom knowingly, as they both realized that maybe Dr. Beele's relationship with Dr. Bellflower was a bit more involved than just being colleagues in the business of running museums.

"I apologize for not being able to greet you properly upon your arrival," Dr. Bellflower said as she motioned the group to sit around the table. "I had planned for a much calmer, more cordial introduction," she added, as she poured tea for everyone and brought out a tray of croissants and small breakfast pastries.

Hieronymus smiled at her warmly. He then set about introducing the entire team to his colleague. Tom, Elly, AJ, Vic and Lynni all smiled and nodded as their names were called and they made eye contact with Dr. Bellflower. The good doctor returned each smile and nod and refilled all of their tea cups.

"So then, my Detroit guests, maybe you can help me understand what has happened at my museum this morning?" Bellflower began as she sat across from Hieronymus.

The Detroit curator responded with a deep breath, as if what he was going to say would be full of lengthy, detailed description, "You, Ms. Bellflower, have just had the displeasure of experiencing the Nain Rouge first hand."

The head of the Museum of Science and Industry gave Dr. Beele a bemused, dissatisfied look, "Perhaps you could provide a bit more detail, sir?"

Beele smiled coyly and began once more, "I'm so sorry, yes, quite right. As you know, we came here to meet with you and the other knights of the order to discuss the strange and disturbing disasters that have befallen our nation in the past few weeks. I explained in my letter to all of you that I believed Lutin, the Nain Rouge, to be the cause of all of this trouble. I had no idea that we were being followed. When we arrived this morning, the docents came running out to our van and brought us in to find your museum in shambles…and you unconscious."

"But why my museum, and why me?" Dr. Bellflower wondered

aloud.

Elly interjected, "Lutin had been trapped in Detroit for centuries. He had cursed the city, but in the process, had become part of the curse himself."

"Yeah," Tom added, "Elly and I found out that the curse was tied to the first settlers of Detroit and the land around the city. The settlers kicked him out and he cursed them. He told them:

'Take what you steal and steal what you keep
The shepherd must pay for his sins with his sheep'."

Elly broke into the conversation, "Tom and I found out that we were the last descendants of the first French settlers, so the curse fell on us. We were the ransom to the curse. So, if we died, the curse would be complete – Lutin would rule the land once again."

"But they tricked him!" AJ exclaimed, as he slid forward in his seat. Everyone was a bit surprised as AJ was usually the quietest in the group. "Tom and Elly got the Nain Rouge to cross over the city line, outside of the city limits. He melted! I saw the spot where it all happened."

"It's all true," Tom confirmed, "The only down side was that when we broke the curse, we thought it was all over. Boy, were we wrong. A

~ 37 ~

month ago, all the bad stuff started up again… and it was even worse this time."

Elly added, "It looks like when we broke the curse, Lutin didn't die – he was just released out into the world to cause more trouble."

A look of guilt fell across the faces of both Tom and Elly. They couldn't help feeling that they were at fault somehow. Everyone else in the room sensed their shame too.

"Come now," Dr. Beele said firmly and clearly, "What's done is done. Tom and Elly acted heroically in defeating the Nain Rouge once. If it wasn't for them, he would have taken over the water and land already and none of us would be here."

"That is quite true," Dr. Bellflower smiled reassuringly, "Such bravery from ones so young. That goes for not only Tom and Elly but for all of you. I am both thrilled and comforted to have you here with me today. Now that I understand what has brought us all here in this moment, I am confident that this is the right group to accomplish the task at hand."

"To be sure, Maggie, to be sure," Dr. Beele concluded. "Now we better check into our hotel before the meeting of the Knights of the Order of the Garter is called into session. We will all need a good rest to undertake what is about come.

Chapter 7
Gas

Dr. Margaret Anne Bellflower led her new companions out of her executive offices and down the employee elevators. As the elevators opened up onto the main floor of the museum, the entire troupe was enveloped by the dull darkness that permeated the unlit exhibit halls.

The clustered group weaved slowly through the museum, being careful to avoid any fallen objects or overturned artifacts. As they were nearing the north doors, Elly stopped suddenly and looked over at Tom, AJ and Vic, "Guys, that's really gross, c'mon, stop it."

"What the heck are you talkin' about El?" Vic shot back, a little annoyed.

Elly shook her head and tried to be a little more discreet, whispering under her breath, "Um, that smell…like someone has a rotten egg in their back pocket."

All of the boys looked at each other, back and forth, in complete denial. Despite her efforts to keep her conversation private, everyone could hear the dialogue between Elly and her male counterparts. Dr. Beele and Lynni looked at each other and chuckled a bit as they walked to the exit.

"No wait!" Dr. Bellflower shouted in a way that stopped everyone in their tracks. "I smell it too, and it's not coming from over here!"

The whole group began sniffing at the air, in an effort to pick up the scent that Elly and Dr. Bellflower had uncovered. Gradually, the entire entourage began nodding their heads and saying, "I smell it too," at different intervals.

"That odor is not from any teenager," Dr. Beele concluded, "It smells like natural gas to me. That is a distinct odor, indeed. Pure, natural gas is colorless and odorless. I have been told that this odiferous scent we are now sharing comes from a chemical added to natural gas for the purpose of detection."

As Dr. Beele finished his assessment of the smell, an unnatural rush of foul wind blew through the museum. Everyone covered their mouths and coughed violently as they were nearly overcome by a woozy wave of rotten eggs.

"It's a gas leak! We've got to get out of here!" Dr. Bellflower screamed. "This place could blow up any minute!"

"Maggie, where is the gas shut-off valve? We may still have time…" Dr. Beele gently grabbed Dr. Bellflower by the arm, "You get the children out to the street. I will shut the gas off."

"The main valve is right below us, down the stairs, over there on the right, but it is too dangerous…"

Without warning, before Dr. Beele could make a move to the basement stairs, Vic bolted to the right and was already making his way down into the basement.

"Vic, no, wait!" Dr. Beele had lost all of his composure and was screaming for the teen to come back to the group. Just then, another blast of foul air exploded into the main hall. There was no way to get to the basement stairs now. Dr. Beele corralled Margaret Anne and the rest of the teens and herded them outside as quickly as possible.

~ 41 ~

Down in the darkness of the basement, the air was actually much more fresh and clear. Fortunately, Vic had kept the flashlight from his earlier excursion through the museum, in his back pocket.

He looked up and saw a series of pipes running back and forth across the ceiling of the basement. For the first time, he was glad he had helped his dad remodel the family room last summer. Despite his attempts to avoid hard work at all cost, Vic had learned a little bit about electrical wiring, plumbing and heating when working with his dad. He knew that a gas line looked different than a water line. He also knew that the shut-off valves would be different too.

Even though the pipes were a lot bigger than ones you'd find in a residential home, Vic was able to figure out which was which, and he began to follow the gas pipe along its route under the museum.

"I hope I'm going the right way," Vic muttered under breath. He had no idea which way led to the main valve. He just had to guess at which direction to turn and hope for the best.

What started as a slow walk along the pipeline transformed into a jog and then a full sprint. Vic just had a feeling that he was headed in the right direction. Fortunately, he was right. After a few minutes of running, he stopped directly in front of a gray cinder block wall. Running up and down the wall were large pipes connected with valves, gauges and compression dials. The gas valve was clearly marked

"MAIN" and Vic breathed a sigh of relief.

Upon closer inspection, however, the teen realized that the handle on the main line had been snapped off. It looked like something or someone had twisted the valve so violently, that it stretched and bent in an elongated fashion, until it finally gave way and twisted off.

After a brief moment of panic, Vic smartly walked backwards, staring above at the gas line he had just passed. A few feet down the line, he happily found an auxiliary valve with the handle still intact. The valve turned rather easily and soon, the gas was shut off completely.

As Vic made his way back upstairs, he could already sense the air was clearing. Upon reaching the main hall, he could hear a great commotion, as if the entire building was swarming with panicked activity. The hall was filled with masked firefighters, paramedics and utility workers, all scrambling around. Some were looking for stranded staff that may still have been in the building. Others were looking for the source of the gas leak that had caused everyone to evacuate.

"Are you okay, son?" a firefighter asked Vic, his voice muffled through his mask. He was quite surprised to see Vic walking upright around a hallway that was still half-full with invisible, toxic fumes.

"I'm fine," Vic coughed.

Without another word, the firefighter wrapped his arms around

~ 43 ~

Vic's shoulders and hustled him briskly out of the museum.

A crowd had gathered in the back of the museum parking lot. The rescue worker guided Vic to the corner of the lot, where he was reunited with all of his friends.

"Vic!" Elly and Lynni yelled as they came running toward him. "We're so glad you're not – well, we're just so glad to see you!"

"Don't worry, I know what you guys meant…I'm glad I'm not dead either."

Tom and AJ came up right behind the girls. They were as concerned as everyone else; they just didn't think it was very cool to jump on top of him the minute he returned. Maybe it was just a guy thing, but the other boys could tell Vic appreciated them holding back a little, based upon the way he was squirming with the girls hugging and pawing him all over.

Tom patted Vic on the shoulder, "Hey, I'm glad you're all right man, really."

"Yeah, what happened in there?" AJ added in wonder.

"Well, I just reacted, I guess. Before I knew it, I was down in the basement looking for the shut-off valve. I didn't know the fumes would get that bad. Kind of stupid, huh?"

"Stupid and brave," Tom corrected him.

"The weirdest thing was that when I found the valve, it was

snapped off. It looked like someone with one powerful giant hand had twisted the handle hard – so hard that it yanked it right off!"

"That is strange…" Dr. Beele's voice floated over the top of the teens' conversation. "I must commend you for bravery Vic, but admonish you for your impetuousness. That was a dangerous thing you did."

"Sorry, doc, I guess I just didn't think," Vic apologized.

"Well, lucky for us your instincts were spot-on. The firefighters informed me that if you hadn't shut off the gas when you did, the entire building would have exploded. I shudder to think what would have happened then."

"All's well that ends well," Dr. Bellflower stepped up reassuringly. "Let's not fill the boy with 'what-ifs' and 'almosts', Ronnie. We all have been through enough and it is not even noon yet. Let's just be thankful we are safe and sound."

The teens looked at each other and smirked a little. The subtle grinning soon turned into muffled, repressed giggling. As if in unison, the group of youths blurted out, "Ronnie?!!"

Dr. Beele's face turned a deep crimson as the tension of the moment was broken with deep, heart-felt laughter. It was just the release that everyone needed. Without ever saying it, the entire entourage knew that the Nain Rouge was the cause of this near-disaster. Things were getting worse and the darkness seemed to be rolling in much more rapidly.

The council meeting at the Union League Club was not until tomorrow morning. Secretly, everyone was hoping and praying that nothing else would happen before then. Though they all suspected that hoping and praying would probably be of little help right now.

Chapter 8
Subtle Changes

***I**n 1891, a* high-pressure gas deposit was tapped in central

Indiana, and a 120 mi pipeline was built to bring the gas to Chicago, Illinois. By the year 2000, there were over 600 natural gas processing plants in the United States connected to more than 300,000 mi (480,000 km) of main transportation pipelines. These facts meant very little to people on the surface. Never before and never again would those above ground care so much about the pipes that lay beneath them.

The hotel parking attendant was not too happy about having to valet park the museum van. A vehicle of that size posed a problem equal to the biblical task of passing a camel through the eye of the needle. Regardless, Beele did not mind the dirty looks or grunts from the attendant, for he had much more weighty matters on his mind at that moment.

There seemed to be an inordinate amount commotion around the city as they had driven to their hotel. In the main lobby, strange commotion and anxious activity permeated the cavernous room.

The curator from Detroit approached the front desk, "Good Day, we are checking in this afternoon. May I ask, is there a convention here today? I noticed a great amount of hustling and bustling about the hotel."

"No sir," the desk clerk responded, "Everyone is talking about the explosions. Didn't you hear?"

"You mean the gas leak at the Museum of Science and Industry?" Dr. Beele answered nervously.

"No, that was just a gas leak," the clerk continued, "I'm talking about the explosions that happened all around the country…all near museums too…how weird is that?"

"Very 'weird' indeed." Dr. Beele replied, as if he had been put into some sort of a hypnotic trance. He was trying to sort out and process everything that he had just heard.

The curator took the room keys and guided the troops up the elevators and into their rooms. Beele was ominously quiet the entire time and all of the teenagers knew that something else was happening. Despite their questioning, Beele waved off their requests for more information, indicating that now was neither the time nor the place for such conversations.

After freshening up a bit, the entire group gathered in Dr. Beele's suite. Everyone was anxious to learn what heavy matters were weighing on Beele's overtaxed cranium, so they waited quietly.

The television was on and the twenty-four hour news channel was broadcasting stories of destruction and mayhem from all around the United States. The teenagers couldn't help but be sucked in to the baritone reporter's broadcast, as he announced:

"A panic-stricken nation braces itself against a rash of natural gas explosions. Museum districts around the country are reporting strange natural gas leaks, with some leading to fires and explosions within the buildings and surrounding areas.

Gas explosions at The Cole Land Transportation Museum in Bangor, Maine and the Everhart Museum in Yuma, Arizona have yielded the greatest casualties. Emergency crews are reporting several people injured and five fatalities at these remote locations.

Authorities fear that the prevalence of these leaks and explosions in more heavy-populated areas may result in more injuries and fatalities..."

Elly's mouth opened slightly as she watched the T.V. in horror. "He's making it happen. He's connecting the grid..."

"All those people...just innocent people..." Lynni said to herself in a faded voice of drifting sadness.

Vic, Tom and AJ were staring at the television as well, though they seemed too entranced to say anything. Everyone in the group knew that they were on a mission to stop Lutin. They just had no idea how powerful he had become. What began as an adventure of empowerment and excitement was rapidly turning into a helpless excursion of danger and despair.

~ 50 ~

Dr. Beele's voice floated from behind the youths and rested in each of their ears, "These are grave times…" his words were filled with an ominous anxiety that sent a shiver down the teenagers' spines, "…and grave times bring out the best and worst in people. I am fortunate that these events from the past few months have brought out the best in all of you." Beele's tone had moved away from its foreboding sounds into a warmer, more reassuring melody.

"Yeah Doc, but look what's happening now!" Vic pointed to the television, "This is bad Doc, really bad!"

The curator suppressed a quick, anxious response and let Vic's statement float in the air for just a little while.

"I cannot deny what you are saying, Vic. In fact, I think that you are spot-on in your assessment of the situation. This is what Lutin wants. He wants to create fear and panic across the country. He's using natural gas as one of his agents of evil. What better way to do it than a pyrotechnic display within the cultural centers of major cities and small towns? I suspect there is even more to it than that. Has anyone else noticed a slight change in things since we were evacuated from the museum?"

The teens looked around the room at each other and then back at Dr. Beele.

"What do you mean by 'change', Dr. Beele? Elly asked as if she was already in deep thought about his choice of words.

"How do you feel? All of you?" Beele questioned again.

"I don't know," AJ responded first. "I guess a little scared, a little angry, um, and maybe a little depressed."

"Yeah, me too, pretty much the same as AJ…" Tom added.

Elly, Vic and Lynni nodded in agreement. They were all feeling the same way without really knowing it.

"Ok Doc," Vic asked the curator directly, "what's going on that you're not telling us?"

Hieronymus Beele furrowed his brow slightly and stroked his chin gently, "I believe that he has released the energy from the ground."

"What energy?" Lynni asked anxiously.

"The negative energy, Lynni. The evil power that has been trapped underground for centuries – Lutin is releasing it through the gas lines."

"How can you be so sure?" Tom wondered aloud.

"I am not so sure, Tom," Beele replied, "but from what I have seen, it is all beginning to make sense to me."

At that point in the conversation, the wise curator asked his young friends to think about what happened *after* they left the museum.

Tom remembered the rescue workers being very helpful at first, but once they knew that everyone was safe, some of the workers began complaining about people being ungrateful, how dangerous their jobs

~ 52 ~

were and how they never got paid enough money to do the work that they did.

Elly thought about the trip over to the hotel. Even though they were in a big city like Chicago, the drivers seemed more aggressive and unfriendly than any she had ever seen. People were leaning on their horns and shouting at other cars and trucks to get out of the way.

Then there was the hotel lobby. AJ remembered that just a few minutes ago, they were all standing in the middle of chaos. At first, he thought that the commotion was caused by the news of the explosion at the museum. But after what Dr. Beele said, AJ began looking at the scene in the lobby with a much different perspective.

"Guys, downstairs, in the lobby, remember?" AJ tried to jog everyone's short-term memories, "There were people fighting and arguing about a bunch of different things, I heard some of what they were saying and it wasn't about the museum explosion."

'You're right, man," Vic added, "I heard people fighting too. Now that you mention it, it seemed like they were fighting about a bunch of dumb stuff too, like who's going to pay for the cab and whose morning paper got taken from the breakfast table in the lounge."

"Ladies and gentlemen," Beele interrupted, "I believe these happenings are the direct result of Lutin. What you have been witnessing is the direct result of the negative energy that the Nain

~ 53 ~

Rouge has released all over the country."

"But how does he do it?" Lynni asked. "I know he's trying to connect the energy grid, but how does releasing negative energy from the ground make it happen?"

"I think I know," Elly said quietly but thoughtfully.

In the recesses of her brain, Elly remembered the dog-eared page from the Earth Science textbook that revealed some of the Nain Rouge's secrets to her and Tom back in middle school. She could actually see the text on the page in her head:

"The earth's natural electromagnetic field has a frequency measured as about 7.8 Hz or Hertz. This is documented in the Schumann Resonance measured daily in seismology laboratories.

People give off electromagnetic energy as well, their brains emitting alpha frequencies of 7 to 9 Hz.

The human brain in a relaxed state will have the same frequency of vibration as the energy field of the earth".

"Lutin is releasing the negative energy under the ground to create an imbalance," Elly stated clearly.

"An imbalance?" Lynni asked again, "An imbalance of what?"

Tom chimed in, "Yeah, Elly's on to something here!" He stood up from his seat and clearly agitated and excited. He knew where Elly was going with her thought processes. "We saw something in our science book a few years ago, that said our brain waves, our thoughts, and our energies are tied to the energy in the earth. It said something about balance. When our energy is in balance with the earth, we will feel happier and relaxed…"

Elly finished Tom's thought, "And when our energy is not in balance with the earth, we often feel angry or depressed."

"I do believe that you are on the precipice of solving this riddle," the curator acknowledged.

AJ pointed out to the group, "Maybe Lutin's trying to create that imbalance of energy, then?"

Vic jumped up as if something had clicked in his brain, "That's it! That is how he'll connect the grid! He'll dump all of this negative energy around the country until everything is saturated with it! With everyone off-balance and in a bad mood, the negativity will just keep growing and feed upon itself."

"I am afraid that you are all correct in your assessments of the situation." Dr. Beele said calmly. "Lutin has discovered humanity's greatest weaknesses – pride and ego."

Now Tom seemed a bit confused. He thought that he had the whole thing figured out until Dr. Beele threw that curve ball at him; "What does ego have to do with it?"

"He is feeding our greatest weakness, Tom," Beele answered curtly. "The negative energy that has been released creates a negatively-charged field all around us. This field is always there, along with a positively-charged field. Under normal circumstances, the positive and negative forces balance each other out, but Lutin has changed the game.

By flooding the world with all this negativity, he has created an environment of evil. This evil seems to be seeping into all of us, feeding our basest desires and fertilizing the bad seeds within each of us. Our egos will deny that this dark energy even exists. Our pride will rationalize it away and allow those shadowy seeds to germinate and flower within us. These are the black blossoms that the Nain Rouge has been cultivating for centuries. The season is right for planting and I fear the harvest will be fruitful."

The curator delivered his speech in a trance-like, prophetic state. The teenagers had nothing to say. Something inside of each of them told them that Dr. Beele was right.

What were they to do now? The damage had been done and the process of transformation had already begun. They had seen it with their own eyes – the hearts of people were changing and not for the better.

Perhaps the Knights of the Garter had an answer. Of course, that would have to wait until morning. It was this time before dawn that seemed like the longest wait of their lives.

Chapter 9
The Union League

T*he DIA van* pulled up to 65 West Jackson Boulevard. A stately gray building rose before them. Their view was interrupted only by the slight flapping of a giant American flag, waving gently above the main entrance.

Established in 1879, the Union League was founded to uphold the sacred principles of citizenship, to promote honesty and efficiency in government, and to support cultural institutions and the beautification of the city. Like any club, the Union League had its secrets. Now, 11 of those secrets were waiting for the 12th to arrive.

Beele pulled into the parking garage located next to the Union League building and eased the van into a larger parking spot normally reserved for delivery trucks and limousines. As he went to unlock the vehicle's doors for the teenagers, he found that the automatic button was stuck. The doors wouldn't open. He tried to push the door open with his shoulder, but to no avail.

Vic saw the curator struggling with the driver's side door and made an aggressive attempt to pry open the side door of the vehicle, pushing at it with all 125 lbs. of his teenage force.

The doors would not budge.

Then, without warning, a dark, crimson figure thunked hard on the hood of the Econoline van – BOOM!

"Greetings, fellow travelers!" a snide voice slid right through the front windshield like a foul, muffled breeze, "I trust that you are enjoying your stay in this wonderful city?"

"Lutin!" everyone seemed to yell in simultaneous surprise.

As the group stared at the copper-colored troll sitting on the hood of their vehicle, they couldn't help but notice how he had grown in size and stature since their last encounter. The Nain Rouge looked more powerful than ever. His scrawny, stubby arms and legs seemed to have grown. There were noticeable muscles on all of his appendages. He also appeared less slouched and curled up than before. There was a menacing vitality in the way he sat upright directly in front of them.

"Let us out!" Lynni yelled in fury and panic, "Now!"

"As you wish, child…" Lutin said dismissively.

With that, he waved his hand and the door locks popped open. Vic reached for the door handle immediately, but it was burning hot. The handle singed his fingertips and he cried out with a painful yelp. Lutin smiled with fiendish glee and slid toward them from the hood of the vehicle, seeping through the front windshield like eerie liquid smoke. With great deft and dexterity, he stepped onto the dashboard of the van, sitting comfortably in front of his captive audience.

"What's the matter?" Lutin chided, "Did you change your minds? How sweet, that you wish to stay and chat with me for a while."

"Stop messin' around!" Vic yelled, "You can't keep us here!"

"Whether I can or cannot keep you here is irrelevant," the Nain Rouge responded coldly. "In fact, all of you are irrelevant. The changing times are upon us and there is nothing that any of you can do about it. Do you think these explosions and disasters are the end of it? Ha! They are just the beginning…"

Lutin sat up and stood on top of the dashboard, pulsating red with power and energy.

"How pathetic! You thought you could catch me, Lutin, by following me around the countryside in an old truck? You are more ridiculous than you could ever know!"

Lutin's arms were pumping up and down and his head was oscillating wildly, back and forth.

"I cannot be stopped! Soon, humanity will feel what I have felt for the past three hundred years. Soon, the hatred, the anger and the pain will be yours to wallow in like the sad little pigs you are." Lutin smiled with great satisfaction, "And do you know the most delicious morsel of it all? The fact that you and your kind are doing it all to yourselves."

Lutin looked right at Tom and Elly. He had vowed not to reveal any of his intentions ever again, yet somehow, he felt that Tom and Elly might possess some secret knowledge like the last time they confronted him. The Nain Rouge's eyes glowered deep into the teenager's faces. He was searching their expressions, their thoughts for anything that might expose any unseen information that could be used

~ 61 ~

against the red dwarf.

The teens knew better, though. They refused to meet Lutin's glaring red eyes with their own. Instead, they hung their heads down, nearly pressing their chins against their chests.

"Oh, the clever lambs have grown shy," Lutin mocked them. "To no avail young ones, the dice have been cast and your futures are in the rubbish heap with the rest of your kind. Breathe deeply my friends, there is freedom in the air!"

On that bizarre, unsettling note, the door locks of the vehicle closed and opened in violent repetition as Lutin vanished in a confusion of sulphuric smoke.

Like deer in the high beams of an oncoming Jeep, all of the occupants of the van sat stunned. Though the events that just occurred took only a few minutes in real time, it seemed like they'd been trapped for hours inside of the vehicle. Lutin's presence had a strange way of twisting time into disorienting and surreal knots.

Dr. Beele broke the frozen trance with a clarity that blew the smoke out of everyone's brains, "Let's get inside now, we needn't keep the council waiting any longer."

The dizzy troupe fell out of the van and stumbled slightly on their way to the main entrance of the Union League Club. The spinning of the heavy, brass revolving doors only added to their disorientation, as they soon stood huddled together in the front lobby of the old, stately building.

The lobby of the Union League Club stood in stark contrast to our weary, wobbly travelers. There was nothing weary or wobbly about these grand surroundings. Enveloping the group were the polished dark mahogany moldings, checker-tiled floors and heavy wet plaster walls that echoed the strength, endurance and fortitude of old Chicago. There was an honorable energy in the club; an energy that seemed to have been created over generations, by souls that sought something better for humankind.

This was just the kind of energy that Dr. Beele, Tom, Elly, Vic, AJ and Lynni needed to revive their spirits. It was as if they had found sanctuary from the negativity that continued to grow throughout the rest of the country.

"May I help you?" a friendly voice said from behind a dark oak desk.

It was the first friendly voice they'd heard since meeting Dr. Bellflower back at the museum.

"Yes, you may," Dr. Beele replied with a bit of hesitation, "We are looking for the meeting of the National Art Council."

"Yes sir. That would be on the third floor, in the St. George Conference Suite."

The desk clerk escorted the party of six across the grand lobby to the waiting elevators. Soon, the slightly shaken group was on their way upstairs to meet the other Knights of the Order, masked by their professions as art scholars and experts in antiquities.

The elevator was old and slow. What it maintained in traditional style and grandeur, it lacked in speed. The ride up to the third floor seemed to take forever.

"What do you think Lutin meant when he said we were 'doing it to ourselves'?" Lynni broke in from the back of the Otis lift.

Elly wondered as well, "Yeah, we know that he's releasing the negative energy all over the country, but why would he say that we're the ones doing it?"

"Maybe he doesn't want to take responsibility?" Vic conjectured.

"No, that's not it," AJ answered. "I don't think the Nain Rouge cares a bit about responsibility. Actually, I think he gave us a clue without even knowing he did."

"What clue?" Tom asked.

"He just confirmed what Dr. Beele said about how the negative energy is spreading. This is the clue that shows us how Lutin will complete the grid." AJ seemed quite sure of himself and the rest of the group listened intently. "When we're exposed to the bad energy, we can either fight it or fall to it. Most people will fall under its power without even realizing it. I'll bet when that happens, it just creates more negative energy. He's using us like bees to pollinate our own black flowers, cultivating our own destruction!"

"It's like a virus, a disease! It will grow and spread no matter what we do!" Elly added as it clicked in her brain.

"A pandemic of evil..." Beele blurted out with an exasperated breath of horror and helplessness. "The natural gas is just one agent that's bringing the negativity to the surface. Once above the earth, the bad energy will spread like the flame of a torch, passed from one branch to the next. The flames will multiply without ever losing their original strength, growing more powerful and destructive until the entire world is engulfed in an inferno of invisible fire."

With a weakened sigh, Beele wondered quietly how or if the growing flames could ever be extinguished.

Chapter 10
The Art Council

The elevator doors to the third floor finally opened into a Victorian-style hallway complete with rose-colored, flowered wallpaper, antique upholstered chairs and a claw-footed coffee table.

Dr. Margaret Anne Bellflower was standing in the shadow of the conference room door, welcoming the group into the large and well-appointed room.

"Ronnie, children, welcome!" Dr. Bellflower stepped out of doorway and beckoned the group into the large, conference room. She seemed to have regained the glow and luster in her cheeks that had been drained out in those dark hours in the museum. Her cheery demeanor had a strengthening effect on Tom, Elly, Lynni, Vic and AJ. Even Dr. Beele appeared a bit more at ease as the entire entourage made their way around the large oval, mahogany table to the six vacant chairs that were waiting especially for them.

As they walked around the table to their seats, they caught the eye of every individual already seated in their designated chairs. On the table, in front of each person, was a name card that identified each Knight of the Order. The teens scanned all eleven names, trying to gather in the information quickly, without staring or appearing rude:

Martin Mulholland – Albuquerque, New Mexico
Lilith Fairchild – New York City, New York
Malachi Randolph – Scranton, Pennsylvania
Wilson Gartner – San Francisco, California

~ 67 ~

Karen Scofield – Atlanta, Georgia

Julianne Lynn – Charlottesville, North Carolina

Bertram Bernhard – Los Angeles, California

Kevin Stickley – Seattle, Washington

Cheryl Jones – Cincinnati, Ohio

Hollis Graveslee – Nashville, Tennessee

Nancy Feinstein – Dallas, Texas

Once seated, a few minutes were set aside for formal introductions. With each passing face, Tom, Elly, Lynni, Vic and AJ felt that they were in the company of greatness. They couldn't quite put their finger on it, but something about this collection of people created such a strange force within the room, that the darkness that had previously permeated their thoughts seemed to slip into the pale shadows of the room.

Each introduction came with an odd smile and an acknowledging nod of the head from every member of the council. When Dr. Beele's turn came, he too spoke with a soft, reassuring tone that only added to the growing oddness inside the room.

Now it was the teens turn to introduce themselves. They were more than a little nervous. It was very intimidating to speak directly to such an esteemed group of knights, professors and scholars. Tom began the introductions with a curt nod and an uncomfortable, crooked smile. Elly, Lynni, Vic and AJ followed suit, simply stating their names and nodding humbly in front of the council. Each nod from the children was greeted with a thin smile in return, providing a lukewarm sense of security or reassurance.

With the introductions and pleasantries properly exchanged, Dr. Bellflower began, "Well now, should we all get down to the business of the day then?"

"Excuse me, Maggie," Dr. Beele gently interrupted, "Before we begin, I think everyone should know about our confrontation in the parking garage just a few minutes ago."

"Ronnie, don't tell me you were accosted?!" Dr. Bellflower acted as if Dr. Beele had been attacked by a mugger or a street hoodlum of some kind.

"Well, in a manner of speaking, we were all accosted – by the Nain Rouge."

An audible gasp filled the room as the council shot glances back and forth between Dr. Beele, the children and themselves.

Dr. Gartner of San Francisco questioned, "What's the meaning of all this, Beele? Do you mean to tell us that the Nain Rouge is here at the Union League Club at this very minute? "

Hieronymus replied with great clarity, "No, the Nain Rouge

~ 69 ~

disappeared from view only a short time ago. Please, let me explain. Lutin trapped us in our van down the parking garage as we tried to enter the Union League Club. He inadvertently confirmed what we have suspected all along, that he's connecting a negative energy grid around the entire country."

"Does he know about us? About our council meeting here?" Dr. Jones from Cincinnati asked with a sense of deep concern and slight panic.

"If he does know about the council, he did not say. But what he did say was something quite curious and puzzling. He stated that we are doing this to ourselves".

Vic interrupted quickly, "We think he's talking about the negative energy. As he connects the grid, we're the ones who are spreading the negativity from one person to another!"

The council stared at Vic as if his interruption was one of impertinence and rudeness.

Lynni added, "It's like a disease that's spreading without anyone noticing!"

The faces of the council turned very grave and deeply serious. Private conversations sprung up between council members in the form of whispers and subtle tones, covered with cupped hands over hidden mouths. Their eyes moved back and forth from their mumbled rumblings, onto the teens and Dr. Beele and then back to their hushed discussions. This went on for a very long time.

Beele spoke quietly to Dr. Bellflower as the teenagers wondered aloud amongst themselves what all of the chatter could be about. After a few minutes, Dr. Beele nodded to Dr Bellflower and began speaking again, "Friends, colleagues, let me be direct and to the point. Prior to this meeting, I had briefed all of you on the circumstances that lay before us. These dark times have necessitated that we all convene as a group. We are here to define some solution, some answer to the problems that Lutin has created."

Beele's voice slowly became more forceful and compelling, as if a certain amount of frustration and anger was brimming causing it to rise to the top of his throat and then to the tip of his tongue. "Whispering and private, unsolicited sidebar conversations serve only to further Lutin's cause!"

A hush fell over the room as Beele's voice continued to rise in both pitch and amplitude, "This should be a time of unity – not a time of gossip and conjecture! You may know of the events that have led us to seek your counsel and strength, however, you know nothing of the personal pain and human suffering that these children have faced at the hands of the Nain Rouge!"

It was as silent as an empty church. The Knights of the Order were dumbfounded. The teenagers were stunned. No one, not even Margret Anne Bellflower, had ever heard Dr. Beele raise his voice in such a manner. She stared over at Dr. Beele for only a brief second, blushing slightly at the rush of tension and excitement that his powerful speech had induced in her.

Martin Mulholland of Albuquerque, New Mexico was the first to regain his composure, "Now see here, Hieronymus…"

No sooner had the knight spoken, than he was cut off by Dr. Bellflower, "No, Dr. Beele is absolutely correct. We have no idea what our guests have been through. Far be it from us to question anything that they say. Our role here is to listen, to support and if possible, defend against the dark forces that are now swirling all around us."

It was at the very moment that everyone in the room realized what was happening. Lutin was right. They *were* doing it to themselves. The field of negative energy that the Nain Rouge had created had permeated the Union League Club and infiltrated the very room in which the counsel was meeting. Any negative thought, any feeling of fear or distrust was now amplified and expanded into the rising flood of darkness.

But the speech from the Detroit curator had broken the spell – at least within that room. That message of truth, so clear and clean and direct had sliced through the negative energy.

~ 72 ~

Elly spoke up, "Can you feel it? Can you feel the energy changing?"

AJ joined in, "I feel it! It's like the tension is loosening. There is calm now, a more relaxing feeling."

It was true. The anxiety and pressure that had been building up over their short time together was now dissipating. It was as if a pressure valve had been opened up and the dark steam had been released from the room. Sunlight, like the sound of bright harp strings, began to slip through the rectangular windows that framed the outside wall of the meeting room.

Hieronymus spoke once again, "So, I see now that it can be done."

A puzzled look fell over the faces of the exhausted council members and the teenagers.

"Please Hieronymus, we are all spent and even more confused," Dr. Feinstein pleaded, "We're sorry that we were overcome by the invisible darkness too. I fear that we offer little help to you and your friends. So, what do you mean by 'it can be done?' "

"This was a test." Dr. Bellflower stepped in. "Yes, I see it now. Ronnie, you were testing all of us, weren't you?"

"Yeah," Tom concluded, "You knew the darkness was here, all around us. We could sense it, but you knew for sure. You wanted to see if we could fight it, beat it together as a group, right?"

~ 73 ~

"You are half right, young Tom." The curator continued. "Upon entering the room, I could feel the negative energy all around us. We have, however, been surrounded by it since our mishap at the museum, so that was no surprise. What was surprising was how aggressively the energy was affecting our hosts as soon as our meeting began. As the tension grew, I felt I had no other recourse but to speak my mind freely and directly. Frankly, at that point, I did not care what the results were; I only wanted the truth to be heard."

Lynni piped in, "It was the truth that freed us."

Dr. Beele smiled at her. The words of his favorite poet and artist, William Blake, rushed through his head, as he responded, "When I tell any truth, it is not for the sake of convincing those who do not know it, but for the sake of defending those that do."

It was clear now. The Nain Rouge could be fought. The negative energy that he was releasing could be diluted and weakened…maybe even destroyed. They had been able to break Lutin's spell on them, which was a great sign of hope. It was on a small scale, in a single conference room, but it did happen.

Yet, a bigger question remained. How could they help the rest of the country? How could they spread a message of truth and positive energy faster than Lutin could release evil?

It seemed the work of the Knights of the Garter had just begun.

Chapter 11
To Tell the Truth

S*o what is* truth?

This was the question that dominated the rest of the meetings between the Knights of the Garter and the teenagers from Detroit. How was this small band of do-gooders supposed to spread positive energy around the country in the form of truth? Is that what was going to defeat the ever-growing power of the Nain Rouge?

For the next few hours, there was a deep, philosophical debate about the meaning of truth. Dr. Beele pointed out that the negative energy dissipated only when he expressed his feelings directly to the group. So was that the truth, the willingness and strength to express one's feelings?

Dr. Malachi Randolph of Pennsylvania argued that truth was not about expressing one's feelings. Randolph asserted, "If we are to defeat the Nain Rouge, we must first agree that truth is based upon defining real events and facts, not opinions and feelings. We need to be objective about this and come to the same conclusion together."

"Dr. Randolph, I disagree wholeheartedly," came a Nashville twang from across the room. Hollis Graveslee stood up and faced Dr. Randolph. "Malachi, I have been sittin' here listenin' to y'all postulate about truth, philosophizing about what that word means, and it seems to be beatin' around the bush, if you ask me. The way I see it, if you believe that there's only one truth, and that you're the only soul in the world in possession of it – well that's the root of all evil. That's what Lutin is counting on. That's how he wins."

"I think that you're both right – in part," Dr. Bellflower said as she deftly, yet graciously inserted herself into the conversation. She got up from her seat at the table and directed her attention to everyone in the room. "Friends, I think we are over complicating the issue here, which is precisely what Lutin would like us to do. Even with the best brains in this room, there is no way in which we are going to define an abstract concept like truth – that should not be our charter anyway. We are here to stop the Nain Rouge. To do that, we need to uncover his weakness and exploit it."

All eyes in the room were now directed on Margaret Anne Bellflower. It was as if she was cutting through the confusion and chatter, peeling away the layers of conversation to reveal something for which everyone had been looking; "For our purposes here, truth is a combination of both head and heart. In our heads, we know that the Nain Rouge is physically releasing his negative energy into the world. Once his grid of evil is complete, his power will be unmatched. Now in our hearts, we know the effects of this energy. It causes us to snipe, bite and snap at each other, which in turn, creates more negativity. This is how the evil is spreading."

"Spot on, Margaret!" cheered Professor Lilith Fairchild. "You have arrived at the point directly. Truth is at the same time conditional and eternal. It remains constant though its appearance may change throughout time. The truth is shaped by our unique circumstances, but its spirit remains the same. Our truth, here today, is to fight this evil by expressing the depth of our feelings for human kind, and for each other."

"Precisely, Lilith." Bellflower agreed, "Dr. Beele shattered the darkness by expressing his deep feelings for our young guests. This depth of caring was a physical manifestation of truth and love – that is what broke Lutin's spell and brought light into the room."

Tom, Elly and the rest of the teenagers knew in their hearts that the Knights of the Garter finally understood now. All of their big words and lofty ideas had resulted in the revelation that the only way to combat the Nain Rouge was through tangible expressions of truth. That was the illumination they would need to pierce the veil of creeping darkness that continued to wrap itself around the country.

It was time to take action. It was now time to fight – to fight harder than they'd ever fought before.

Chapter 12
Sir Gawain

"*Friends, our time* together grows short," Dr. Beele began after many hours of deep discussion. "It is time for resolve and resolution. I do think it to be of the utmost importance that we remember the charter of our order – the Garter of Truth that drives us all."

Lynni wondered aloud, "Dr. Beele, what's the Garter of Truth?"

Beele began again, "An excellent question Lynni. I would think this to be a critical and highly appropriate time to share with everyone the story of our founder - Sir Gawain."

"For those of you that don't already know, Sir Gawain was a knight of the round table in King Arthur's Court. During a New Year's feast, he was challenged by an uninvited guest; a strange, green knight, who dared someone from the gathering to cut off his head with his own axe. If the challenger was successful, he would be named the victor. If he failed, he would have to meet the green knight again in one year's time. The green knight would then return the blow to the challenger's neck.

King Arthur was about to accept the terms of this challenge, but Sir Gawain stepped in at the last minute and took the king's place.

When Sir Gawain struck the green knight with the axe, his head came off immediately – with a single powerful blow. Then, after only a brief moment, the strange knight picked up his severed head and put it back on his body, as if he was completely unharmed.

Now Sir Gawain was forced to live up to his side of the bargain.

After a year, he had to travel (through great trials and tribulations) to the green chapel to meet his adversary. During his journey, he stayed at a castle, where his honesty was tested three times by the lord of the castle, Bertilak de Hautdesert. He had agreed to share anything he received during this time with Bertilak, but he withheld a garter, given to him by the lady of the castle.

Upon leaving the castle, he finally met up with the Green Knight. As fate would have it, the Green Knight was actually the castle keeper, Bertilak, who had uncovered Sir Gawain's untruth and dishonesty.

When the time came for Sir Gawain to receive his blows from the axe, the Green Knight missed him intentionally on the first and second blows and then grazed his neck with the third, drawing a small amount of blood from the back of Sir Gawain's neck.

With that small dark mark, Sir Gawain was sent back home, wearing the green garter as a sign of his shame and dishonesty."

Dr. Beele paused for a moment to catch his breath. It was at that point in the story that Vic interjected, "Doc, that doesn't sound like much of a brave knight to me. He hit on a married woman, lost the bet, lied and then had to go home defeated. So why model yourself after a loser like that?"

Malachi Randolph stepped in before Beele could speak, "It's what happened when he got home that changed Sir Gawain's destiny, and

~ 81 ~

our history, young man."

"Precisely." Beele had recovered his breath, "When Sir Gawain returned to King Arthur's court, he was hailed a hero. He was a hero, not so much for his pure nature and for meeting the objectives of his quest, but for his ability to endure despite all of his flaws. Yes, despite his human failings, he eventually told the truth and was willing to own up to his mistakes. King Arthur saw these traits of humility, perseverance and forgiveness as admirable qualities that should be retained by each of his knights."

Randolph added, "The garter that had initially been worn as a symbol of shame and defeat, became a symbol of human truth, solidarity and triumph over our inevitable human weaknesses. That is why our order exists. That is why we are here."

There was a feeling of general acknowledgement and agreement in the room. The other knights appreciated how Dr. Beele and Dr. Randolph had been able to convey the true meaning of the Order of the Garter with such depth and clarity. The teenagers seemed to embrace the words that had just been shared with them. As they looked around at each other in silent unity, they felt as if they were now sharing a deeper connection with the entire council.

Before anyone had too much time to reflect upon the stories and conversations, Dr. Beele's face lit up like an incandescent bulb. His expression changed from his usual calm, pensive look to one of agitated excitement. Nobody was quite sure what to make of this middle-aged man, now scrambling through his brown leather briefcase like an adolescent boy who had forgotten where he'd put his homework from last night.

"A moment, please, if you will!" the Detroit curator yelled out to no one in particular.

"What is it Ronnie, what's wrong?" Margaret Anne Bellflower asked as she came over to calm the curator down.

"The book! The book! It's all in the book!" Beele shouted out, with his head deeply buried within his luggage.

Before Bellflower could react, Dr. Beele popped his head out of the leather case, wearing a grin laced with great satisfaction and delight, "Aha! I've found it!"

Within the curator's hand was a small, ratty-looking book that appeared to be very old.

"*Le Prince Lutin* from 1697!" Beele affirmed as he dropped the book down on the conference table with a satisfying SLAP!

"What in the blazes are you talking about, Hieronymus?" Dr. Stickley of Seattle questioned.

"See here, Kevin. This book, this French fairy tale that I have had for so many years - it is the key.

~ 83 ~

Beele glanced over at the teens. "When Tom and Elly first came to me a few years ago, I referenced this book in my search to explain the Nain Rouge. In fact, here is the passage I found..." Dr. Beele opened up the book and began to read the words that rang quite familiar in Tom's and Elly's ears:

"You are invisible when you like it; you cross in one moment the vast space of the universe; you rise without having wings; you go through the ground without dying; you penetrate the abysses of the sea without drowning; you enter everywhere, though the windows and the doors are closed; and, when you decide to, you can let yourself be seen in your natural form."

A chill ran through Elly's body, "Dr. Beele, we already know that stuff about Lutin, so what's the big deal?"

"The big deal, my dear, is in another passage from the book that I never read to you before. Its significance has always puzzled me...confounded me for years, until this very day. It speaks of how one might deal with Lutin, should he ever cross one's path." Beele read the following passage aloud for the entire room to hear:

"Give what you took
And return what you stole

~ 84 ~

The nightmare will end
With release of your soul.”

There was a long pause in the room. Nobody really knew what to say or think.

"So, what does it mean, Ronnie?" Dr. Bellflower said softly.

"It's in response to Lutin's first curse on Detroit. It's how we defeat him."

Tom stood up quickly and spat out, "Dr. Beele is right! Lutin himself told us about the curse he put on us, our forefathers and Detroit! When they kicked him out of Fort Pontchartrain, he told them,

'Take what you steal and steal what you keep
The shepherd must pay for his sins with his sheep.'

That quote from Dr. Beele's book must link directly back to the original curse!"

Elly added with equal amounts of energy, "It all makes sense now! The shepherd doesn't actually have to pay for his sins with his sheep – he just has to tell the truth, to right the wrongs of his past."

"Lutin lied to you then," Lilith Fairchild stated matter-of-factly.

"Of course he lied," Dr. Beele interjected, "He is evil and the lord of lies. By believing his untruths, these children were pulled right into his trap and almost paid for it with their own lives."

"So, now what are we supposed to do, Doc?" Vic added with AJ and Lynni wondering along with him. "How do the few people in this room make the world right again? How do we make up for the screw-ups our ancestors made? It's impossible!"

Hieronymus Beele leaned back in chair, almost far enough to lift the two front legs off of the ground. He stroked his chin thoughtfully, before slowly leaning forward, "You have come to the crux of the problem, Victor, my boy – the very crux. The answer to your questions is simply this - we will lead by example to change the hearts of humanity.

We must be the keepers of truth who spread its light deep into the darkness."

Chapter 13
The Storm Upon Us

***A**ll hell had* broken loose.

In that short time within the Union League Club, it was as if the cardboard cut-out of society had come unglued. Phones were ringing off of their hooks, as each member of the Order fielded calls from around the country, documenting floods, minor earthquakes and multiple tornadoes. Outside the window of their Union League conference room, they could hear hail, pelting the building like small chunks of concrete thrown down from the sky.

Even worse, were the reported crimes against humanity. Each knight learned of the rapid rise in crime, theft and fighting in the streets of their regions, towns and neighborhoods. In some cases, the National Guard had been called out to put a stop to all of the insurrection.

People reported seeing the Nain Rouge too, though they had no name for the little red creature that danced with delight near each disaster or mishap. Seeing him didn't seem to matter anymore. It was as if he was everywhere all at once. The damage was being done whether people believed in him or not.

It was time for the meeting of the Order of the Garter to adjourn. The winter break from school was almost over and Tom, Elly, Vic, Lynni and AJ had to get back home. Even though they all really wanted to help, they knew that the problems with Lutin were now far beyond their abilities alone. It would take a group effort, a greater force of good to combat the evil that had been unleashed on the country. The plan of action had been agreed upon by the entire council, like Dr. Beele had suggested.

The truth would be revealed through the museums.

Before the final recess of the council, the Knights of the Order of the Garter had acknowledged that the seeds of distrust and evil had been planted in multiple places over the course of human history. The artifacts of human existence now resided in museum collections all around the world.

Dr. Bertram Bernhard of Los Angeles pointed out to the group, "Our museums, our centers of culture and learning are filled with objects of historical and artistic significance. I must admit, however, and with a sense of growing shame, that a number of these objects were obtained from sketchy dealers or by less reputable means. I have no idea where some of our pieces belong. Our archives are filled with artifacts that originated from unknown sources."

There was a general consensus from the group that all of their museums may be filled with historic items that may hold the seeds of untruth and evil.

Dr. Scofield from Atlanta added, "As curators of the collections in our respective museums, the responsibility falls upon us to validate these objects. We must reveal the truth about these items, even if it means exposing fakes, forgeries, or objects that have been obtained

~ 89 ~

unfairly over the centuries."

AJ had been sitting for hours, listening to the Knights of the Order go back and forth on all of these topics. Thoughts had been swirling through his teenage brain and he finally had to say what he'd been thinking.

"Maybe that's why Lutin started with the museums – those are the places where the best part of humanity is on display. Our history is scattered throughout your halls for everyone to see. It's just that we never saw the bad stuff – but Lutin did. He knew what was there all along."

AJ was right, and the Knights of the Order were quick to admit it. In fact, there was a firm agreement by the council to quickly try to rectify the situation in an effort to subdue the Nain Rouge. The plan was put down in writing and agreed upon with a unanimous decision.

Each curator would head home to their region of the country. They would work within their museum networks to find the truth about their collections and artifacts. Once they had done their research, they would announce their findings to the public, opening the doors of each museum for everyone to see the truth – uncovered.

Margaret Anne Bellflower took the written plan and reviewed it with the group once more. They committed it to memory. Upon final approval, Dr. Bellflower folded the thin sheet of paper and lit it on fire with a long stick match. As the plan burned in a large ceramic ashtray in the middle of the conference table, each Knight of the Order knew that their time had come.

Through the subtle smoke and ashes that rose up and curled darkly in the air, the faces of the council expressed a singular, determined thought.

It was time for battle.

Chapter 14
Moving Shadows

Lilith Fairchild left the Union League Club quickly. She pulled her car out of the parking garage onto Wacker Avenue. She had scheduled an early evening flight back to New York, where she would begin her difficult mission to set up an exhibit that would purge her museum of negative energy.

As she headed out to Chicago's O'Hare airport, she could feel the negative power all around her. Through the rain and hail that had been constantly pelting her car, she could sense the bad attitudes and anger of the other drivers and the pedestrians that shuffled through the wet, cold streets.

The traffic light was yellow, but she was sure that she had enough time to get through the intersection.

A quick glance in her rearview mirror sent a sudden shock of terror through her entire body.

"Good day Lilith," came a cold, slithery voice from the back seat of the sedan. "In a bit of hurry, are we?"

"Lutin!" Dr. Fairchild yelled, "Wha – How – What are you doing?!"

"I should ask you the same question – Doctor!" Lutin shot back like a viper, spitting venom. "I'm quite sure that your desire to get back to New York so quickly is not due to homesickness. As a Knight of the Order you are duty bound to battle me at every turn. And that is where you will find your efforts futile!"

Dr. Fairchild had completely forgotten that she was driving. The appearance of the Nain Rouge was such a shock, that her mind seemed to go into a trance, where she was totally unaware of her surroundings.

Suddenly, there was the sound of horns and screeching brakes everywhere.

CRASH!

BOOM!

THUD.

The airbag had exploded directly in Dr. Fairchild's face, preventing her head from flying through the windshield of her car. The front of the vehicle was completely smashed in from the light post she had just rammed into. She'd made it through the intersection but the distraction from the Nain Rouge caused her to lose control of the steering wheel, sending her onto the sidewalk and into the heavy steel street light.

A few people were now gathered around the smoldering, smoking car, trying to pry open the driver's side door to get Lilith out of the wreckage.

Once she was safely on the curb, she noticed that only a few people had stopped to help. Strangely, the rest of the drivers and pedestrians continued on their way, as if nothing had happened. Lilith was sure that this was another effect of the negative energy that continued to spread across the country. The incident had left her with mixed feelings of sadness and hope.

She was sad that more people weren't willing to stop and help a fellow human being. But her hopes were raised by the handful of strangers that had fought off the negative energy all around them and proceeded to do the right thing by offering her assistance in her time of need.

Strangely enough, similar scenes were playing out as the other council members left the Union League Club to return to their regions.

Martin Mulholland's plane had to be rerouted on its way back to Albuquerque, New Mexico. The pilot made an emergency landing when someone claimed they saw a small, red creature pulling off one of the electrical panels on the wing of the plane.

Malachi Randolph got caught in a terrible snowstorm. It came out of nowhere, as he drove across Indiana and Ohio on his way back to Scranton, Pennsylvania. He was stuck on the roadside for an entire night until help finally arrived almost a day later.

Wilson Gartner was stuck in Chicago. He decided to stay put for a while, as the earthquakes in San Francisco were now too numerous and too powerful to enter back into the region.

Karen Scofield made it back to Atlanta, but when she got home, she found that there had been a terrible fire. Many of her prized belongings had been burned in the blaze and she was left with little more than a smoldering shell for a house.

When Julianne Lynn got back to Charlottesville, North Carolina, she found her dog and cat had run away. They were nowhere to be seen. Fortunately, she found them a few days later, scared, clearly having been frightened by something. They had been hiding in the woods at the end of her street.

Bertram Bernhard also made it back to Los Angeles, but he felt that he was being followed the entire way home. It was as if a dark shadow kept looming over him everywhere he went. It didn't matter if it was dark or light out, the shadow never seemed to leave him.

Kevin Stickley finally returned to Seattle. His return trip was prolonged by a terrible case of the flu that hit just him before he left Chicago. On a layover in Denver, Dr. Stickley had to be driven to the hospital, where he laid for days, in a deep stupor from his illness.

Cheryl Jones drove back to Cincinnati with her engine smoking constantly. She too claimed to have seen the Nain Rouge, hitchhiking by the side of the road with an eerie grin and a long, gnarled finger that pointed directly at her as she passed.

Hollis Graveslee had to call one of his friends to retrieve him from the Union League Club. At the end of their last meeting, an incredible fear overcame him and he was unable to leave the conference room. Despite everyone's best efforts, he would not get up from his chair at the table. Eventually, Dr. Graveslee, his chair and his luggage were transported back to Nashville. He had to sit upright and alone in his chair, in the covered bed of a pick-up truck that his friend had driven up from Tennessee.

Nancy Feinstein took the train back to Dallas. During her journey, an odd little waiter offered her a complimentary cup of black tea. She didn't remember much after that, only waking up in the Dallas train station with a dizzying headache and her clothes slightly dirty and torn. Her jewelry and luggage were missing as well. The only thing that remained was the strange taste of sulphur and almonds lingering in mouth for days after her journey.

It was clear that the knights were off to a very poor start in battling the Nain Rouge. If these first few days of the fight were any indication…the war was far from over.

Chapter 15
The Return to Motown

Winter break was over, and Dr. Beele and his group of teens needed to get back to Detroit and Royal Oak as soon as possible.

School was starting again on Monday and Hieronymus Beele needed to marshal his troops at the Detroit Institute of Arts for the largest and most controversial exhibit of his life. Tom, Elly, Vic, Lynni and AJ were completely worn out from their harrowing journey. There was almost a sense of relief that they didn't have to shoulder the whole burden of battling Lutin anymore. The battle had begun, but they were no longer alone.

The plan the Knights of the Garter had formulated was for each region of the country to bring all of the artifacts, objects and works of art out of the archives of the museums throughout their network. The true history and origin of these objects would be presented to the public. This meant that any work containing a sketchy or dark past would be revealed in its entirety, as honestly and truthfully as possible.

These exhibits would be launched simultaneously around the country in hopes that the positive spirit of forgiveness, understanding and acceptance would break the spell that the Nain Rouge had cast over the land.

All of the presentations would be marketed and presented with the title:

The Red Truth Exhibits.

The greatest challenge that faced all of the knights and their friends was time. Time was running out. The Nain Rouge had a death grip on the entire country. It was as if the grid he had created was now wrapped around the entire country. Like a fisherman's net cast out wide along the water, evil was pulling people in, snaring souls like unsuspecting fish being pulled to shore in angry, anxious bunches.

As the museum van crossed into Detroit for the first time in a week, there was a feeling of both anxiety and relief for the weary travelers.

Dr. Beele would spend a great many days in the basement archives of the DIA, working with his team of curators and conservators to catalogue and validate each object for the Red Truth Exhibits.

In the darkly lit archive rooms, a small group men and women labeled artifacts to be displayed in the exhibit. Each item needed to be researched, tagged and cleaned before it would be ready for presentation to museum patrons in a few weeks.

The scene in the basement of the Detroit Institute of Arts was being played out all across the country. Every museum within the network was preparing for their own Red Truth Exhibit, identifying, tagging and cleaning objects from their own collections.

The process was slow. In every city and town, curators were running into problems and issues with getting the exhibit together. One day, the lights stopped working and the power went out. The next day, the heat shut off and filled many museums with a creeping cold that froze the curators' hands and fingers. Some selected artifacts even disappeared, only to reappear in the men's bathroom or behind a coat rack in the main lobby. Yes, strange happenings became the norm for these dedicated workers; despite all the problems they faced, every museum trudged on with preparing the Red Truth Exhibits.

Tom, Elly, Vic, Lynni and AJ returned home on Sunday afternoon with barely enough time to prepare for school the next day. Nearly all of them had forgotten that they had a term paper due by Wednesday of that week. Ironically, the topic of the paper was to be a discussion of the impact of Art on modern society. Each of them could certainly put a new twist on that subject – if anyone would believe them.

The shortened weekend evaporated into nothingness; and sooner than to be expected, the teens found themselves in the familiar halls of Royal Oak High School.

Only now, things seemed completely different.

"Doesn't this feel weird?" Lynni leaned over to Elly as they stood by their lockers in the hallway.

"Yeah, it's weird Lynni, but get used to it – we're in high school," Elly replied matter-of-factly.

"No, you don't get it El – everyone seems even weirder than when all this stuff started. Nobody talks to each other. All I ever hear are people mumbling under their breath. They don't even look at you when you say, 'Hi.' The best I got today was a grunt from Steve DiPalma!"

Just then, Tom, Vic and AJ came up to the girls.

"Is this spooky or what?" Vic butted in.

Elly and Lynni gave Vic a look like they had no idea about what he was talking about – but they knew exactly what he was talking about.

"Why is no one here hanging around after class?" AJ wondered aloud. "It's like, everyone just goes to class and then goes home… very creepy if you ask me."

"Guys, we all know why this is happening," Tom pointed out as he looked around the empty halls. "The negative energy has taken hold. It's gotten even worse since we left for winter break. Man, I hope Beele and the others can make their plan work… I just wish we could help somehow."

Chapter 16
The Basking Dwarf

L*utin sat inside* his sewer filled with great comfort and satisfaction. His plan was working to perfection. The negative energy grid was almost complete and soon he would have complete control of the entire country, and then the entire world.

He chuckled quietly to himself, "The fruits of my labor have finally ripened. How wonderfully delicious it is to sit here in my new-found glory and splendor, while those humans flop around above me like panicked fish on a wooden dock – how I love to watch them gasp for air!"

Lutin gingerly adjusted his seat against the slimy sewer wall, happy with the thought of the darkness that continued to descend upon the world. He knew that his time had finally arrived and that it would be impossible for anyone to turn the tide against him.

"They've had this coming for a long time," he said to himself, "I tried to be nice, tried to be helpful, cordial…but their egos…their greed…their selfishness; these are the blankets they have chosen for their beds."

Lutin then thought about the Knights of the Garter. He knew what they were up to. It didn't matter anymore. Their efforts were so weak and futile that it only served to tickle his wicked brain. In his corrupted mind, he was unstoppable.

With that warm and reassuring thought, Lutin flew out of the lowest level of the sewer to the surface streets above, penetrating the walls, brick and concrete with ghostly ease. He was now happily resolved to take a personal view of the destruction and mayhem that he had caused around the entire country.

In an instant, the Nain Rouge was in the air, traveling faster than the speed of light. Streets, houses, and cars flew past him like the blurred wings of a floating hummingbird. Mountains, rivers and fields approached and departed from Lutin's gaze in only an instant.

Despite his rapid journey, the Nain Rouge was magically able to view all the scenes that played out on the ground below him. With crystal clarity, he could detect the crumpled houses that had fallen into great gaps in the concrete, caused by recent earthquakes. Lutin gushed at the sight of hundreds of cars and trucks being swept away by the raging floodwaters of rivers overflowing their banks. He was filled with glee, watching a cluster of tornadoes rip through corn and wheat fields, chewing up everything in their path.

But the greatest, most satisfying spectacle for the evil little dwarf was the people. As he gazed down upon the land and water, he saw numerous people, men, women and children in various stages of turmoil. Some were arguing over parking places at the local mall. Some were fighting about whose turn it was to watch the children. And some simply watched and refused to help others who had been hurt or who were in need of some assistance.

Lutin took all of this in. Like a deep breath of stale, foul air, the Nain Rouge inhaled all of the evil and negativity that continued to blossom around the country.

As with most things in the world of the Nain Rouge, Lutin eventually began to grow tired of his travels. He became more and more curious and he couldn't help but wonder what was happening with those meddlesome teenagers and that ineffectual curator from the place where he was once imprisoned. He couldn't help himself. He needed to see the sullen, sad masks of defeat, hanging from the faces of those who thought they could overcome the power of the Nain Rouge.

"I think it's about time to pay my friends a last visit – one final taste of victory in the land of my making."

On an imperceptible wisp of putrid air, Lutin was gone again, heading back to the city and the straits were his new reign over the land and water would begin.

Chapter 17
Let's Make a Deal

The *early March* skies over Detroit were strangely calm and blue, as the Nain Rouge broke through and crossed the border of the city. It had been a long while since he had penetrated the invisible wall that once held him captive for so many years.

Now, he could come and go as he pleased. No longer was he bound to the land that he had once sworn to protect. No longer was he a prisoner to his own curse, the curse that unwittingly locked him up in the city for over three hundred years.

It was with great satisfaction that Lutin was able to slither under the streets and through the sky at his own will. He revelled in his new-found freedom, a freedom that grew along with his increasingly evil power.

Yet, as he slid up from the sewer onto Woodward Avenue, he felt different. Something wasn't right.

"Hmmmm…" he thought out loud to himself, "there is something different about this place now. What is wrong here?"

Lutin took a walk around the neighborhood. He was barely noticed by the heavy foot traffic along Woodward near Midtown and Wayne State University.

Students shuffled from class to class in the late winter cold with barely an acknowledgement of each other or Lutin. This pleased the Nain Rouge. He could see that his negative energy was still permeating the people here like it was across the rest of the country.

Still, something did not sit right with the red dwarf. The bad attitudes of the people seemed just fine, but where were the natural disasters? There should have been more flooding, tornadoes and power outages. This unsettled the Nain Rouge and heightened his anger, anguish and paranoia.

"I'll pay a little visit to the good doctor to see what he is up to. It's too quiet around here, if you ask me."

In an instant, Lutin was slipping through the front doors of the DIA, discreetly making his way down the marble steps to the basement archives. When he reached the entryway door, the Nain Rouge creaked it open just a little, in order to spy on the activity that was taking place in the rooms beyond. Dr. Beele looked up for moment when he heard the noise, but resumed his work when he could see nothing of substance in the doorway.

To Lutin's surprise, he could see the makings of grand exhibit being put together by Beele and his team of conservators. There were objects from all different time periods, in many different styles and mediums.

"So, this is their plan to defeat me? An exhibit?" Lutin laughed loudly. He shuttered and spit and guffawed like a braying donkey – hee-hawing at the top of his lungs. He laughed so loudly, in fact, that Dr. Beele stood up and looked around the room with great surprise.

With his spectacles firmly pressed on to the end of his nose, he cried out, "Lutin! I know you are here! Make yourself known!"

The Nain Rouge stepped out into the light, away from the boxes and crates, from where he'd been eavesdropping.

"Oh, Dr. Beele!" Lutin oozed with false apologies, "I'm so sorry to disturb you in your important work!" Lutin looked around at the artifacts and scoffed.

"What brings you here?" Beele demanded of the red dwarf.

"Curiosity and comfort," the Nain Rouge replied with a long, snide, biting grin. "I was curious as to what you were working on and comforted by the fact that my work is nearly complete.

"You're a fool if you think humanity can be overtaken so easily," Hieronymus shot back at the red dwarf.

"Oh, am I?" Lutin chuckled. "See for yourself, it's playing out right in front of you – right in front of them and they don't even know it!"

With a great sweep of his little arm, the Nain Rouge began to generate a vortex around both the good doctor and himself. A great whooshing of wind filled the archive room and before Dr. Beele could utter another word, he found himself flying up and out of the basement toward the great coved ceiling of the main hall. Beele shut his eyes tightly as he braced for a powerful impact with the hard, white plaster of the museum's inner roof.

~ 110 ~

The impact never came.

Instead, Dr. Beele and the Nain Rouge penetrated the many layers of the DIA ceiling with great force and speed. With no effort of their own, the two dark figures were lifted skyward, beyond the trees, rooftops, and antenna towers of the city. If anyone had bothered to look up (which they didn't), they would have only seen two tiny specks in the sky, probably mistaken as lost balloons or maybe two small seagulls making their way across the river to Canada.

Eventually, the tiny tornado slowed its spinning and gently set the doctor and Lutin on top of the tallest building in Detroit. They were left alone on the lofty roof of the central tower of the Renaissance Center, a group of seven interconnected glass towers that loomed high above the Detroit riverfront.

From this perch, Dr. Beele grew dizzy looking at the land and water that rolled out before his eyes. Yet, despite the great height, he found that there was no wind or noise to trouble him or the Nain Rouge. It was as if the vortex that continued to swirl silently around them had created a comfortable vacuum, allowing both figures to sit, stand or move about without fear of falling.

"Take a look around you, doctor," Lutin offered as he waved his hand again, "As far as the eye can see, the crimes of men and women continue unfettered."

~ 111 ~

Dr. Beele looked south, down the river toward Lake Erie. Astonishingly, his vision suddenly became telescopic. The curator looked down from his airy seat, through the atmosphere, the clouds, and the trees until a small side street came into plain view. On this street, he saw two hooded figures, knocking down a helpless pedestrian and stealing his wallet. It was all right there, as plain as day. It was as if Beele could have reached out to intervene and helped the man who was lying on the ground. But he couldn't. He was miles away, stuck on a city skyscraper.

Lutin then pointed in a different direction, further out of the city. In fact, it was as if he could point to other regions, in the direction of other states and they would be drawn closer to his outstretched finger with the same telescopic effect. The Nain Rouge began to show Dr. Beele images of his dirty work in Ohio, Pennsylvania, Georgia, Texas, Wyoming, California and even as far away as Alaska.

Wherever Lutin pointed, some terrible image of the troubles in the world would play out before the tear-filled eyes of Hieronymus Beele.

"Enough! I've seen enough!" Beele finally cried out. "You've made your point, Lutin. Now, what do you want of me?"

Lutin sat back gingerly on a steel heating duct, "Well now, I've been thinking," the red dwarf stroked his dirty red chin. "I must admit, it has been great fun exacting my revenge on humanity. Yet, as things continue to flow in my favor, I have grown bored of being alone in my glory. I need someone to share it with – a partner in crime, if you will."

"What are you saying Lutin?" Dr. Beele stated, a bit confused.

"Yes, yes, I was just getting to that. As things get progressively worse for your kind, I feel it important to have someone to bask in my glory with me. Over the years, I have watched you Hieronymus. Once I thought you to be an old fool, an imbecile like the rest of your kind. However, you have proven to be an intelligent man; an individual who can truly appreciate the darkness that I have cast over the entire country. When taking all of that into consideration, I have chosen you to be my understudy – my right hand man!"

"You're insane!" Beele blurted out in disbelief. "What would ever make you think that I would side with you?"

"A valid question, my good doctor, and a question I have considered prior to you asking it. Your answer is this – as payment for your friendship and service, I will reward you with anything of this earth. You're a man of the Arts, perhaps an ancient artifact, painting, sculpture or some other object? Actually, you can have as many as you like from anywhere in the world. All you must do is make a pact with me that promises your allegiance...forever."

There was an empty silence after Lutin spoke those words. His

~ 113 ~

offer hung above Dr. Beele like the silent Sword of Damocles dangling precariously overhead by a horse's hair.

"Oh, and there is one more thing I have forgotten to mention," Lutin broke the awkward silence. "If you come with me in loyalty and service, you will prevent this!"

Just then, the Nain Rouge pointed his finger in a northerly direction. In an instant, am image of Royal Oak High School came into view. The school was empty, except for five students who were very familiar to Dr. Beele. It was Tom, Elly, Lynni, Vic and AJ.

It was clear that something was very wrong at the school. There was smoke everywhere and flames seemed to engulf the outer façade of the building. Hieronymus could see the children in panic, running through the smoke-filled hallways in an effort to find the exit. He could hear them screaming for help, as if they were in the next room.

"So, what is your answer?" The evil dwarf asked softly. "Your time is running out, doctor, as is the time for a few others that you seem to care about."

Beele spun around quickly and put his nose directly against the gnarled nose of the Nain Rouge, "My answer is NO!"

No sooner had Beele said those words than the images of the high school, the fire and the trapped teenagers vanished.

There was a great sucking sound, as the vortex that surrounded them sped up again. In less than a second, Beele was whooshed back down into the DIA, back into the basement archives and dropped on the cold tile floor.

"Blast you Beele!" screamed an angry voice that emanated from the basement walls in all directions.

The curator rubbed his head, still feeling dizzy from his harrowing journey. Lutin was furious that Beele had found him out and called his bluff.

It was all a trick.

"You and your stupid exhibit will fail!" Lutin's disembodied voice echoed through the corridors of the archives. "You will all be destroyed!"

Hieronymus now knew that his friends were fine. The Nain Rouge had only created the mirage to bring Beele over to his side. Everyone was safe, for now, but the exhibit was in greater danger than ever.

Lutin had full knowledge of what the Knights of the Garter were trying to do and he would stop at nothing to defeat them.

After a few minutes, the red dwarf's screams finally faded from the curator's ears. Yet the cold shiver of his words resonated inside his head like the chanting of hooded monks in a dark, sinister monastery.

Looming shadows of doubt were beginning to overcome Dr. Beele's deep conviction and belief in goodness. They wrapped themselves around his head and heart in a slow, suffocating constriction until he could think of nothing but failure and disappointment.

Maybe the national exhibit was a stupid idea; an idea that would never work.

Chapter 18
Opening Day

March came in like a lion and was going out like an even more ferocious beast. The weather around the country had become more foul and unforgiving than when Lutin had begun his reign of fear and terror.

It was clear that the Nain Rouge was growing stronger every day. The fact that he was now aware of the Red Truth Exhibits only made matters worse. Though he thought the knights' plan to be laughably weak, Lutin could not help but feel a little nervous about how the public might react to such a presentation of humanity's mistakes, flaws and shortcomings.

After all, evil could never rest. Any ray of light was a threat to the delicate, dark web that Lutin had cast over the country. It was his job to keep humanity in the dark, unaware of the power of good that every person possessed – if they only acknowledged it.

Sunday morning came, in all of its drab, gray attire with a steady downpour of rain added in for good measure. Tom, Elly, Vic, Lynni and AJ agreed to meet at the bus stop to get down to the DIA early for the grand opening of the Red Truth Exhibit.

Across the country, similar scenes played out, as multiple museums fought bad weather and various other mishaps in order to get their Red Truth Exhibit ready for display. The Nain Rouge was not going to make it easy for any of the museum curators.

In fact, Lutin has his own plan for ruining the Red Truth Exhibits and solidifying his evil reign across the entire country. Huddled under the streets of the city that once confined him, the Nain Rouge sat stewing in the cold, dark recesses of the sewer. For some odd reason, he still preferred the underground dwelling over the fresh air above. He was free to roam as he pleased, yet he still traveled and toiled in the empty, hollow passageways that hid his impish form and disguised his dark deeds.

With only an hour left before the grand opening of the exhibit, Lutin stood up in his desolate cavern, waved his arms slowly, and closed his eyes in deep concentration. An odd, humming sound emanated from his lips, like the sound of a summer cicada, rising in strength and pitch. His body began to glow and pulse with a powerful red light, like a blast furnace in full force. When the noise reached its apex, Lutin's arms shot up skyward with blue bolts of lightning shooting out of each one of his fingers. As he gyrated around his chamber, he chanted:

"Take what you steal and steal what you keep.
This breath is your last, so breathe it in deep!"

Again and again Lutin continued his chanting, increasing his speed and spinning motion with iteration.

Above ground, blue flashes of lightning appeared in the sky for a brief moment, then shot back down, scattering back into the sewers in various parts of the country in a patterned grid. As each bolt of blue light hit the ground, it manifested into another version of the Nain Rouge! Thousands of red dwarves were now rising out of the sewers and heading for the museums that were just about to open to the public.

He was sending out one last blast of evil in his own likeness to stop the exhibits and destroy humanity forever.

It was nearly noon on the east coast, and almost 9:00am in the west. The museums had agreed to open their doors simultaneously, in an effort to generate as much good as possible to combat the spreading darkness.

Within the DIA, Dr. Beele and the children looked out of his office window and down upon the small crowd that had gathered below. They had expected a better turnout, but considering the bad weather, they were not going to complain.

In Chicago, Dr. Bellflower stood in the main hall of the Museum of Science and Industry, anxiously awaiting the opening of the doors. All around the country, curators, museum directors and docents were about to open up their collections for the most important exhibit of their lives – the exhibit to end all exhibits.

Chapter 19
No Entry

At the stroke of noon, the doors to the DIA were unlocked and opened to the waiting public. The crowd that had gathered began to make its way up the steps of the main entrance. Then suddenly, they stopped dead.

From behind the small gathering, a smoky black cloud, like the sooty belch of a coal-driven steam train, rose above the people. It seeped around them, through the arms and legs of the innocent bystanders, coating their clothes with the foul smell of sulphur and tar.

Slowly, it began to take a familiar shape of something not quite human. Dr. Beele, Tom, Elly, Vic Lynni and AJ had all run from the window to the stairs when they saw the smoke begin to billow – they knew exactly who it was.

"Lutin!" the winded group yelled in unison as they reached the main doors of the museum.

The Nain Rouge ignored the cries from Beele and the teenagers. He faced the waiting crowd directly, presenting himself in his true, red dwarfish form.

In a bizarre series of events, identical red dwarves manifested themselves in front museum doors all across the country. They blocked the entrance to all of the Red Truth Exhibits with equal terror and surprise.

On the steps of the DIA, Lutin opened his mouth to speak, while the other versions of himself opened their mouths in complete synchronicity – one voice speaking with many devilish tongues:

"My brethren! You are all being deceived! You have been told that what lies beyond these doors is Truth, but I tell you that what lies before you is Death."

"Anyone who enters this building will be filled with more than a thousand years of human poison.

I have come to save you from this fate – once and for all!"

With those final words, all of the manifestations of the Nain Rouge blew through the front doors of all of the museums. At once, curators, docents and security guards were knocked back into the buildings as the dense fog of darkness swirled into each room of the exhibit. Throughout the halls and the corridors, the people on the outside could hear screaming, howling and wailing like the tortured souls of ten thousand lifetimes.

Beele sat up, watching the rolling thunder of smoke and ash ignite into spiraling flames. He fully expected his artifacts and objects to be completely destroyed in the tumultuous conflagration.

The firestorm grew in size and intensity, continuing to swirl faster and faster around every object in the exhibit. The screaming and the wailing reached a crescendo that could be heard throughout North America. People around the country covered their ears and huddled together in preparation for the end of the world.

Then an odd thing began to happen…

At the height of its chaos, the storm Lutin created began to subside. The fire circled around itself in its own fury, like a smoldering Ouroborus, smothering itself as it swallowed its own snake-like tail.

As rapidly as he had entered the buildings, the Nain Rouge and all of the various versions of himself shot out of each museum. Like charred bolts of lightning – they sparked and spit out the last drops energy onto the cool marble floors and the polished brass fixtures as they passed by.

Something had stopped the destruction.

Lutin's plan to tear all of the exhibits apart had failed for some unknown reason. Now he had to retreat.

The people who were still huddled outside of the DIA saw the plume of thick blackness funnel out of the main doors, evaporating into the giant storm drain under Woodward Avenue.

Lynni, along with Dr. Beele and the rest of the teens picked themselves up off of the floor inside the main hall of the museum.

"What just happened?" Lynni was the first to ask the question that was on everyone's mind.

The curator shook his head in wonder, "I am not quite sure that I know what to make of all this, my dear."

"I think I know," Elly spoke up as she brushed the rest of the soot and ash from her pant legs. "Lutin can't handle the truth."

AJ added, "Yeah, maybe the exhibit couldn't be destroyed because it's all built on truth. His evil can't touch it."

Elly and AJ were on to something. Since the goal of the Red Truth Exhibit was to right past wrongs and bring the truth to the public, it only made sense that Lutin couldn't destroy it.

Of course, there wasn't any time to make sure. The real proof would be if the crowds were going show up and what the overall impact the collections would have on people's hearts and minds. It would take a massive change of hearts to turn the Red Tide of evil that Lutin had created with his energy grid.

The dust had settled and now it was time to welcome the public into the Red Truth Exhibit.

The crowd outside of the DIA had thinned considerably. It seemed that the Nain Rouge's dramatic presentation of his awesome power had frightened away the weak-hearted patrons. Many of them fled during his attack on the museum, leaving only a small line of attendees queued up for entrance into the exhibit.

Dr. Beele greeted each person as they entered the main doors of the DIA. After everyone was safely inside the museum, the curator turned to his young friends and whispered with a twinge of anxiety and hope, "The hour of reckoning is upon us all."

Chapter 20
The Exhibit

*A**cross the country,* the threat of the Nain Rouge had subsided for the moment. Each Red Truth Exhibit opened to the public despite all of the delays.

Initially, only a few people began to file through the artifacts, objects and collections that unveiled the tragedies, triumphs and mistakes that prevailed throughout our human history.

Visitors to the exhibit learned the truth about works of art – how they were created, who cheated the artist and how many people were killed or robbed over the centuries in the effort to retain a particular masterpiece.

Other visitors learned about the Trail of Tears, Japanese Internment Camps and Andersonville – events and places in our American history that brought out the worst traits in our human character. But it was the truth, the truth we needed to face if we were ever to defeat evil.

In every region of the land, people came in contact with the real stories behind the objects and artifacts we had coveted for so long.

Back at the Detroit Institute of Arts, Beele and his young friends observed the tiny crowds with great interest. There were many different reactions that began to surface as people made their way through the exhibit.

Some people emerged from the exhibit in quiet contemplation. Their faces showed signs of deep thought and a resonating wonder at what they had just seen. Other people became emotional. Some patrons left the exhibit crying profusely, unable to control their

~ 127 ~

feelings of deep sadness and grief, pained at the sight of humanity with all of its flaws and failings.

There were even a few patrons who came out of the exhibit terribly angry. Some were disgusted by the display and presentation and gave Dr. Beele a dirty look and a few choice words as they stormed out the museum.

"What a waste of money!" one yelled.

"Who wants to see this kind of garbage?!" another one grumbled under his breath.

"You should all be arrested for showing this trash!" a woman shouted as she shoved open the exit door.

It was true that the reactions to the Red Truth Exhibit were mixed. In other parts of the country, the reactions were exactly the same. There was acceptance, denial and even misunderstanding as people filed through the galleries and halls of each museum.

All of the teenagers and Dr. Beele had been keeping close track of the number of people coming through the exhibit. Though the reactions remained mixed, a funny thing began to happen.

More people were coming.

It was true. What started out as a few curious onlookers was slowly growing into a deeply interested throng of patrons. Beele checked in with the other museums to see how their attendance numbers were doing. Strangely enough, the number of patrons around the country began to grow even more rapidly as the day went on.

Other strange things began to happen.

As the day progressed, there was a subtle change of mood around the museum. Guests began talking to one another more. People began to linger around the displays, instead of just leaving the museum immediately after viewing the exhibit.

Outside of the museum, other changes began to take place. The drab, gray morning burned away into a bright, beautiful afternoon. The streets that once reflected only shadows, slowly warmed with the subtle sunlight of an early spring day.

Soon, the lines outside of the Detroit Institute of Arts began to wrap around the building and run all the way down Woodward Avenue.

Similar scenes started playing out all over North America. Crowds of people were entering the Red Truth Exhibits full of skepticism and curiosity. Yet, they were emerging with some new found understanding, knowledge or revelation – even if some still refused to accept it.

As Tom, Elly, Lynni, Vic and AJ walked around the exhibit hall again and again, they were overcome by the emotion of the moment.

"I think it's working," Elly whispered to Tom as they both watched patrons gather around certain objects and artifacts. Vic elbowed AJ gently in the ribs, as they sat near the exit of the exhibit.

"Did you see their faces?" Vic asked quietly. "It's like they're glowing with a weird energy."

"Yeah, some of them look like they saw an angel or something!" AJ answered, as the two teens continued to critique the responses people were having to everything they saw.

Out in the main hall, Dr. Beele and Lynni were deep in conversation when Tom, Elly Vic and AJ came over to join them. The group had been at the exhibit the entire day. There was only an hour left before the museum would close for the day, yet the lines still grew longer and longer.

"What are you guys talking about?" Vic boldly interrupted Lynni's and Dr. Beele's conversation.

Lynni gave Vic a slightly nasty look, but then shoved him gently on the shoulder, letting him know that she was not really that mad.

"We were talking about the Nain Rouge and the exhibit." Lynni answered. "I was asking Dr. Beele if he thought the plan was working."

"It seems like it to me," Elly added. Tom, Vic and AJ nodded in agreement.

"What do you think, Dr. Beele?" AJ wondered aloud.

"What I think AJ, is that I am not quite sure what is going on. We obviously had a rough start to the morning. In fact, I thought for sure that Lutin would destroy everything. But that didn't happen now, did it?

Since morning, I've been seeing signs of the positive effects of the exhibit. Though people's reactions have been mixed, I do detect a subtle change in the energy around the museum. I take this to be a very good sign…a very good sign, indeed. I have checked in with the other curators and the reports have all been positive and quite encouraging."

"When do you think we will know for sure, Dr. Beele?" Lynni asked with a quiver of worry in her voice.

"Ah, now that is the million dollar question, Lynni. Actually, I think the answer will be a bit more complex than we would all like it to be." Beele stroked his pointy chin, like his next words were to be most thoughtful and profound, "For a very long time, we have set out trying to defeat evil and destroy the Nain Rouge. I have now come to the conclusion that doing so is impossible."

All of teens felt their stomachs drop, like descending that first, giant hill on a roller coaster at Cedar Point.

"Are we doomed, Doc?" Vic abruptly blurted out his concern.

"Not doomed, by any means," the confusing curator replied.

Beele continued, "Let's all think about this for a moment. Tom and

Elly thought they had destroyed Lutin when they broke the curse, but in reality, he was only incapacitated for a little while. When he returned, he was stronger and more powerful, with the ability to move around the country at will."

The teens looked around at each other, knowing that the same thoughts that were running through their collective heads.

Beele went on, "Now we gather to defeat the Nain Rouge by endeavoring to transform his negative energy to good, but what happens? He shows up to destroy everything – and fails. He fails miserably.

So, our plan must be working, correct? We are beginning to see the goodness coming back to the people, back to the regions and back to the country."

"Yeah, our plan is working finally…so what's the problem?" AJ asked.

"The problem lies within this question, AJ, 'Where is the Nain Rouge now'?"

The teens like a number of other people outside the museum that morning, had seen the Nain Rouge vanish in a trail of smoke back into the sewer. Still, without ever saying it, they knew that Lutin was not gone forever, he had only retreated back from where he had started.

Chapter 21
Strange Success

The **Red Truth** Exhibit turned out to be a complete success.

After a rough start, crowds began to show up all over the country to see and experience the exhibits first-hand. As each patron walked through the halls and galleries of the various museums, their moods began to change. In fact, it seemed that the mood of the entire country was changing for the better.

After a few weeks, the natural disasters that had plagued the nation began to subside. The flood waters receded, the tides weakened and the shaken earth that had once quaked and quivered began to settle down into a much calmer state. Slowly but surely, an overall sense of confidence and reassurance began to spring up over many regions across the land.

But the Nain Rouge was not gone.

Amid the newfound spirit and joy that was washing over the countryside, there lurked an all too familiar shadow. Deep down in the sewers of Detroit, sat a faded, gray figure, hunched over and mumbling to himself, "Im-Impossible! Couldn't be done! Shouldn't be done! Wondering, wondering, how have they won?"

Lutin was beside himself with frustration and anger. How did they do it? How could they have foiled his most powerful plan and broken his grip upon the nation? The fact that a few kids and an incompetent professor had beaten him was just too much to bear. Such a small, weak little army to defeat a power such as his – ridiculous!

But it was true. The plan had worked and Lutin's negative energy grid had been broken. Now, he would have to sit and ponder his fate once more. The Nain Rouge would have to wait patiently for his next opportunity to rise again and feed off the bad and destructive forces that humankind has the capacity to create.

"Patience is a virtuous thing, the longer the wait,
The deeper the sting..."

Lutin sang this little song to himself, for some reassurance and comfort to help quell his bitterness and anger. He was willing to bide his time until the next opportunity, when humanity would fall into its bad habits once again. In the mind of the Nain Rouge, it was only a matter of time until people would forget and slip back into their dark thoughts of pride, greed and avarice.

For evil never really dies or goes away altogether. It's always present in this world. That's why it is up to each one of us to be diligent in the lives we lead. We all have the power and the choice to rise into the light or sink into the darkness.

And whatever choice we make, the world will feel its impact.

Chapter 22
The Marche du Nain Rouge

S*pring had come* to Detroit in the form of the annual Marche du Nain Rouge, the parade that led revelers down Woodward Avenue all the way to the river.

An ancient tradition of brooming the bad energy out of the city had been renewed after the victory won by Dr. Beele, Tom, Elly, Lynni, Vic and AJ. The festival hadn't been celebrated in years. But now that the Nain Rouge had made himself known, everyone was more than willing to see him sent back to where he had begun.

This was a celebration to mark the defeat of Lutin and to renew the positive energy that had too long been absent from the city's streets. The small bands of adventurers had been asked to be the Grand Marshals of the first modern day Marche du Nain Rouge. They all accepted with great pleasure and excitement.

"Elly! Look over here!" Tom yelled from across the parade route.

No one could believe it. Each one of them was atop a giant float in a festival that seemed bigger than Mardi Gras in New Orleans. Dr. Beele led the way, as his float, shaped like a golden chariot, chased a costumed character dressed as the Nain Rouge back south toward the river. Beele looked a bit nervous, being pulled by a great white paper-mache horse, so high above the crowd.

Tom waved at Vic and Vic waved at Elly. Lynni's face beamed over at AJ. Everyone waved to the crowd as their floats made their way through a sea of revelers, who threw multi-colored streamers, confetti and beads all along the parade route.

This year, and for many years to come, this was to be a most joyous occasion. A new tradition had begun in Detroit and across the nation.

The cold darkness of winter had ended and the warmth and hope of a new season was beginning. The Nain Rouge was banished again, for at least another year.

Every year thereafter, Dr. Beele, Tom, Elly Lynni, Vic and AJ would be there to celebrate. They would bring their friends and families and everyone would march the Nain Rouge back to the river for another year.

Strange enough, every year the Nain Rouge would be there too. He was much smaller and weaker than he was before. His power had been greatly diminished, but he was there just the same…always present, always watching.

Sometimes, he would watch from the gutter, between the long legs of the onlookers. Other times, he would climb a high building to get a good view of the entire parade. But no matter where he stood, he would always grumble to himself that this state of happiness was only temporary. Lutin would remember the time when he almost ruled the cities, the water, the land and the entire countryside; a time when evil almost won.

But evil didn't win, did it?

This city and its people, like many other people and places around the world found a way to rise above. Back in 1805, Detroit burned to the ground. In the aftermath, Father Gabriel Richard wrote the following words that represent the hope, struggle and perseverance of all people. It's even emblazoned on the city's flag:

"Speramus Meliora, Resurget Cineribus"
(We hope for better things, it will rise from the ashes)

Maybe Elly was right when she said that the good in all of us lasts as long as we want it to last. Every day, we have to make a commitment to try to find that goodness in ourselves, as well as in others. That's how we conquer evil.

Every night before we go to sleep, we can measure our success or failure from the day's struggles. Did the Nain Rouge get the best of us, or did we get the best of him? What's hopeful, exciting, scary and wonderful about all of this is that either way, tomorrow is a new day.

And the battle begins once more.

As evil be to those who evil thinks, so goodness and light come to those who choose to seek it.

The End.

Made in the USA
Charleston, SC
11 March 2015